Growing Up

Free

In America

Bruce Jackson

MANIC D PRESS
SAN FRANCISCO

DEDICATED TO WHAT I'VE SEEN

Cover design and illustration by Tracy Cox
Printed in the United States of America

Library of Congress Cataloging-in-Publication Data

Jackson, Bruce, 1963-
     Growing up free in America / Bruce Jackson.
          p. cm.
     ISBN 0-916397-48-3
     1. United States--Social life and customs--20th century--Fiction.
     2. Inner cities--United States--Fiction. 3. Young men--United States
     --Fiction. 4. Afro-American men--Fiction. I. Title.
     PS3560.A212115G76 1998
     813'.54--dc21   97-45328
                                                         CIP

5 4 3 2 1

Distributed to the trade by Publishers Group West

THE MYTH OF
WESTERN CIVILIZATION

In Exchange For Forty Acres

I own nigger. I purchased it with the blood of my fathers. I stole it from the lips of my masters. I created it in the soul of my sons. It is mine. I am its god. I own nigger, every letter, every syllable. Don't touch it. Don't whisper it. Don't speak it. It is mine.

I own nigger. It defines you now. It reveals you now. It will beat your motherfucking ass now. I own nigger. It don't chain me anymore. It don't beat me anymore. It don't rape me anymore.

I own nigger. It's in me. It is me. I say it. I scream it. I listen for it. I hear it when you look at me. I hear it when the sirens flash, I feel it in the anger of your fist. You want to take this from me. But I own nigger, and I'm holding on tightly. You'll never get it back from me.

The Birth and Death of Action

When he was killed the street erupted for awhile. Time and the fear of pain heal all wounds, but we talked of boycotts, sit-ins, kicking the asses of congressmen, governors, presidents, yeah, we talked. We talked about rising up, burning this motherfucker down, making things right again. Yeah, we talked. We did a lot of talking. Talking made us feel good, better, yeah, talking made it better, almost. He used to think that way. He stopped thinking that way, and when they killed the street erupted for awhile. Our words didn't keep him alive, and we had to say something.

They Say Nigger You Don't Belong Here

They push you away. They look into your eyes, they listen to your voice, they see how fast you can run, how high you can jump, and if you are deemed appropriate, they push you away. They point you in the direction of the stars, they put you on their shoulders. They tell you to stand. They lift until you are larger than they are. Then they push, and they push, they push you away from the fists designed to keep you in the place, they shelter you unscared, black with bodies callused and abused, beaten until hard, beaten until one more scar here or there ain't gonna mean a damn thing anymore, until the only hope for their salvation is to push you away, push you away, they push you away and expect you to rise. They expect you to fly, to take the stars, the sky, to grab hold and bring the world, bring it back, back to the streets, back to the alleys, back to the building made different, made broken, made to define nigger, to maintain nigger, to imprison nigger in a place beyond reach, beyond reach beyond reach unless they push you away push you away push you away to break their chains, push you away to bring the world back, back to their shoulders, back to where it started from.

No Affirmative Action
or
The Niggers Howling at Your Moon

I saw the best minds of my generation run away from oppression in search of hope in a society that despised them, in a society that closed seeing eyes to slide in behind and slit the throats and steal the souls of gifted fools hungry and desperate to believe in ideas diseased with the blood of victims offering salvation from an uncompromising ignorance engulfing what should have eternally been the future.

I saw the best minds of my generation dancing like sideshow niggers to an audience diseased with the love of our ignorance, content to observe and praise the mellifluous composition of our screams, the screams of the young abandoned for the dance, screams of birth metamorphosizin turning angry, festering, exploding upon the streets and alleys and bedrooms of a culture that never tried to exist, that lost its minds to pad its cells to bang its head in comfort, that accepted the drugs prescribed by the man with the awaiting straitjacket and plans of genocide disguised as suicide delivered by ignoramuses and oppressors more than happy to supply the razors that slit the wrists of the mindless masses abandoned by hope, by the future, by the minds strong enough to open eyes.

I saw the best minds of my generation close the eyes that could have opened the eyes that could have led us to the next generation.

There are brutal silences in the night. Listen. You can hear them scream. The sky is a beast of black. The stars are teeth, eating the noise across the street and upstairs, upstairs to the third floor, inside the open door.

"Nigger!" she screams. "Motherfuck you, nigger!" she screams until the fist arrives, until the anger dissipates with contact, with contact, contact, with contact she falls silent, silent. I listen, listen. The silence is brutal.

There are brutal silences in the night. Listen. They're screaming. Black is on fire in the cities below the dark of the sky. Black is inhaling fire, exhaling smoke into basepipe hissing, hissing gapped liquid crack, burning, burning until the hiss explodes, the heart stops and there is silence, blinking silence, silence. I listen. Listen. The silence is brutal.

There are brutal silences in the night. Listen. The sky is attacking. Red and blue lights are flashing, spinning, creating a universe in an alley just beyond listening range. The bullets have been fired. I heard them. You heard them. Hands cuffed unnecessarily rest on ass in backwards prayer as children bathe face first in stains exiting their soul-free bodies, stains creating silence, silence. I listen. Listen. The silence is brutal.

There are brutal silences in the night. You can't stop hearing. I can't stop hearing. It's screaming. It's screaming. We're screaming. Listen. Listen. The silence would be brutal.

A Lullaby to the Nigger Child

"Hush little baby, don't say a word," she screamed while panthers ejaculated black onto the streets of the city, ejaculated black until life was rising mellifluously from the sidewalk, rising newborn from the concrete, from the schools, from the liquor store on the corner, until life was standing, naked and black, hands extended, asking how, asking how until...

"Hush little baby, don't say a word," she screamed, while panthers denied the white in their cum, slapped newborn ass to make the nigger child breathe, to teach the nigger child what black was, what black could be, to teach the nigger child what to do when his dick was hard, what to fuck when his dick was hard, until...

"Hush little baby, don't say a word," she screamed while panthers stuck their hands in their pants to stretch the seams of imagination, stretch the seams of America, stretch the seams of black leather hiding the cum sliding down legs chained at ankles, arms cuffed at the wrist, sliding down moment-old bodies required by law to fight, required by law to fight, required by law to die, to die in spite of M-16s, Saturday night specials, jurisprudence, justice, intelligence.

"Hush little baby, don't say a word," she said, but I don't want to walk white anymore. I don't want to talk white anymore. I don't want to be white anymore. I want to cum. I want to cum. I want to cum and create black. I want to create black.

"Hush little baby, don't say a word," she whispered as she silenced us in the warmth of her breasts, bound our hardened dicks and hid us from the black bleeding from the skies of our cities, hid us from the black falling, beaten back into the streets, the sidewalks, the schools. She hid us until the panthers were running, until the panthers were caged, until the panthers were dead, and my cum could be nothing but white again, and I could hear her whispering her song.

"Hush little baby, don't say a word. Mama's gonna make you a mockingbird, and if that mockingbird don't sing... if that mockingbird don't sing... if that mockingbird don't sing." It must have learned what it was. It must have learned what it cannot be, what it will never be without a fist. It is newborn. We are newborn listening to Mama's song holding us as we close our eyes and sleep until the panthers are a memory fading.

The Necessities of Hell

"Where flames rain with thunder and lightning from clouds drifting in a sky of blue, where the land is charred, but alive and giving birth to the strychnine air we inhale to survive, where the rivers burn to the oceans to light the lengths of horizons kissed by the heat of the moon, where volcanoes erupt the pleasures of winter's cold to children dreaming of, anticipating the joys of ice, where stars are dark to blazing sky, where man would bathe in fire and blacken to cleanse, in a place of life made black with flames, would I be white?" he asked.

"Yes," his father said. "You'd have to be, somebody would have to be white. They'd make you white," his father said.

The Master of Movement

He's a runner. Seems he's always running. His mama would hold him tight, tell him to stop, tell him to slow down, but he was a runner. He was always running. He saw a nigger get killed that way. They hung that motherfucker from a poplar tree down in Mississippi, but he didn't give a fuck. That just made him faster. He's a runner. He's always running. Police don't like that. They arrest niggers for that. They beat niggers for that, toss their black asses in state penitentiary cells too small to run in, too small to run in, but they're never too small to run in. He's a runner. He's always running. Niggers hate that motherfucker. They look in the mirror, and they hate that motherfucker. They give him smack, crack, big dog, PCP. They'll do anything to stop him. Sometimes they drive by and shoot that motherfucker, sometimes they kill him, sometimes they kill him, sometimes they kill everything, but they can't hurt his legs. His legs are always okay, and he's always a runner. He's always got to run. He's always gonna run. "It's raining out," he says, "pouring hot rain." And he's running. His feet will burn in the hell-spit waters of an America stained white if he walks, so he's running. He's a runner. He's a runner, and somebody's gonna get him for that, but "That's alright," he says, "that's alright." He runs. There's no better way to die.

Riding in the Handicapped Seats with That Black Stain in Your Memories

I can see you nigger. Your heart is beating now. It's pumping blood to your veins, and opening my eyes. You are alive now. You are alive. I know your name. I hear your name. It's shouted back to you through public transit windows opened wide enough for you to slip your mouth out to shout a name, shout a name until you are acknowledged, until your name is returned, and you are alive, until you can be seen, until you can be seen and I can see you nigger. I can see you now. Your lungs have air. They've inhaled black. They exhale its sound. I see you breathing. You are alive. You are alive now nigger. I know your name. I see your name. It flows in liquid strokes from paint-filled markers staining the back of my seat on the bus heading inaudibly through your home. It's scratched into confused twists on the streetcar windows, twists as confused as your mama's, your daddy's hand slapping her ignorance into your righteousness, acknowledgment. It's screamed in scribbles washed away at the depot, a nuisance washed away as quickly, as easily as your black ass is washed away from the streets you're breathing on.

And I can see you nigger. I see those brain cells popping. Your hands are moving. Your lips are moving. You are alive. You are alive now nigger. I see you there. I see you there with those bullets coming and your screams ringing out and down that fifty-seat cylinder from the back where your black ass is always talking too loud from, living too loud from, screaming your life from, screaming alive from, and you are alive. You are alive. I see you now, nigger. I see you now as the windows shatter to cross your name from its prominent spot in the ears of our transport through your home. You are alive. I'm listening. I'm listening. Scream that death, motherfucker. We all see you now. We all see you now.

From This Day Forward, No

They hit him with that pipe so hard, they had to yank it out of his skull. He was dead before he hit the ground, but they still set him on fire, and when his body twitched away those last escaping parts of his uppity nigger soul, they kicked his body thinking it still had some life in there. They took a picture. They called it "nigger." They mailed it to our home. Daddy said, "They love to hate." So I asked my mama who to love, and she said, "Love whoever you want to." But when Daddy didn't come home that night and Mama got the mail in the morning, I think she changed her mind.

THE NO SELL-OUT CLAUSE IN THE MESSIAH CONTRACT

Take the bullet, motherfucker. You had to open your mouth. You had to say something. You couldn't let it rest. You didn't let it rest. Now take the bullet. Take the bullet, motherfucker.

Smile when it comes. It's what you always wanted. It's your dream that's gonna put a hole in you. It's your prayer, motherfucker. Take the bullet. Take the bullet, goddamnit.

Everybody's watching now. Everybody's gonna hear your scream. All ears are open now, if you take it. Take the bullet. Take the bullet, motherfucker. Ain't no use in running now. You can never hide again. They're gonna get you sooner or later.

Take the bullet now. Take it while you're on fire. Take it while you're burning the sky. Take it so the world starts a flame from your ashes. Take the bullet. Take the bullet, motherfucker.

Don't you run. Don't you cry. Take the bullet. Take the bullet, motherfucker. We'll know it's a scream if you take it. Take the bullet. Take the bullet, motherfucker, and save us. You said you'd save us all. You're here to save us all. You better save us all.

Poem About a Nigger Who Just Saw Shaka Zulu

King of something. Yeah, that's what I'll be. That's what I'll say. King of some big fucking African country with elephants and lions and shit like that. With some big tittied, nigger black bitches, with two foot afros and them African asses.

Yeah, king of something, something black, something real black, not Bill Cosby black, not Public Enemy black, but chasing down a tiger in an open field and eating it for dinner black, dancing wild by the fire worshipping the moon black, dancing wild by the fire with thirty big tittied, big assed, half naked, nigger black bitches moving in an African celebration of their king, that black, that's the kind of black I want.

Yeah, king of something, something black, the kind of black that makes them niggers on the street get up and say, "Free Mandela! Free Mandela!" But fuck Mandela. I'm the king goddamnit. I got the blood to prove it, the blood, the black blood, the black blood. Yeah, that's what I'll say. That's what I'll be. King of something. King of something, goddamnit.

Keeping Up with the Joneses

When I saw them I wanted to run, but the wind was blowing so hard I could barely stick my leg into that exhaling wall of air, that exhaling wall of nothing, that exhaling wall pushing me. I could barely move forward through that wind. I could not move forward through that wind.

When I saw them, I wanted to run, but the snow came alive and filled the world surrounding me, filled the streets and the alleyways, hid the open windows, the breakable windows. The snow revealed me. It made me obvious. I was that little black spot on their falling sky of white. I was that little black stain on their perfect world of white.

When I saw them, I wanted to run. When I saw them, I wanted to run. I wanted to run so fast I would leave the stains of my skin behind and vanish clean into America. I wanted to run so fast that black would lift in teardrops from my skin and fall unnoticed, unnoticeable through fallen white earth to the parts of the alley beneath the wind, to the parts of the alley where the niggers were, to the parts of the alley where I no longer had to be, where I no longer would be if I could run these stains away.

When I saw them, I wanted to run. I wanted to run through the wind. I wanted to run through the snow. I wanted to run my black away. I had to go faster. I had to go faster. I had to go faster, but the wind is strong when the world is white. Black is obvious when the world is white, and the wind is strong, the wind is strong. There's no way to run. There's nowhere to run, and the black stays, and I stand.

He asked me who was Dr. King, a nigger from the past. We all got a holiday, 'cause someone shot his ass.

He asked who Medgar Evers was, football star I said. Then we watched a baseball game, Yankees 'gainst the Reds.

He asked who Marcus Garvey was, a nigger in a hat, a nigger dressed just like a fool, don't ever dress like that.

He asked about South Africa, I went and got a map. That's just south of Europe, and east of where we're at.

He asked me who was Bobby Seale, I said I didn't know. I gave him books on Washington, and Jefferson, and Poe.

He asked who Huey Newton was, I shrugged and turned away. We watched a documentary 'bout Lincoln freeing slaves.

Then he asked of Malcolm X and that's when I got mad. You keep talking violence, I'm gonna beat your ass. I knew he loved his daddy, he knew I'd tell him right, he knew I'd tell him what to learn, to somehow make him white.

THE NETWORK NEWS

She sings her lies and pushes me, and I'm not falling anymore. I'm moving to her song, to her bewitching melody. I'm getting high, and I'm shocked by the ground when I land.

She sings her lies and caresses me, and I'm not alone anymore. We are making love in her battlefields, fucking to the rhythm of her tomahawk missiles, breeding to the promise of her new world order, and I'm shocked by the blood in my cum.

She sings her lies and calms me, and I don't know the truth anymore. My children are crying. My children are screaming. My children are skinned alive in a hundred million homes by her flickering blue waves, but all I hear are her whispers in my ear, "It's alright, baby. Everything's gonna be alright." Then the Star-Spangled Banner and static til her first morning show.

In Nowhere

In nowhere on a field is a house secluded, a hundred miles distant from any neighbor. Worn, broken, the house stands powerfully, triumphantly. It bleeds the years. It ignores pain to stand in nowhere. I'm going back one day to paint it. I know what color it should be.

SOMETHING LIKE A
POSTCARD FROM HOME

Lethal Doses
for my mother

He was sitting on the front stoop staring down at the street dreaming about any and all of a million thoughts slipping into and out of his mind at the moment. He could do that. He was three years old. He could do that. He could stare out at that street and be anybody that passed. He could stare out at that street and be anything that passed. Dreams blurred into thoughts shaping and he was whatever he wanted to be. His world was a sleeping eye opening as he stared across the street at three niggers bullshitting, halfway through twenty-four cans of Miller High Life, trying to fix an Olds Impala that hadn't moved in any of the three years it took to shape the child across the street staring at the niggers trying to repair a temporary means of escape that probably wasn't ever gonna move again.

A window opened as his mama glanced outside to make sure her boy was in the place he was supposed to be. He heard the sound of wood around glass lifting, and he turned to his mama and smiled. If he wanted, he could get up, take three steps to that window, and touch her. If he wanted to, he could hold her. Mama was always close. Mama wasn't ever too far away from him at this time in his life, and it was okay for him to sit on that front stoop, staring down at the street, staring at the south side of Chicago slowly replacing his dreams with concrete, heart beating to the sounds of sirens crying just out of sight as he tried to ignore the fact that Mama would come running with just a few of his tears, that Mama was allowing him to sit there as long as she could see him, hear him, feel him sitting, as long as sitting was all he did, but staring was all he did, staring, searching for soul, to dream.

Mama couldn't trace his eyes when he dreamed. When he stared down at that street, Mama couldn't see his eyes gliding down the steps to that sidewalk, then five more steps to the pit below the sidewalk, then past the first garbage can to the fifteen-year-old girl lying fetal, on the nod, sleeping awake behind the three other garbage cans in the pit. He was staring down, counting "One, two, three, four" bruises on her legs was as high as he counted, as high as he knew how to count, but there were more. There was a lifetime's worth of bruises running the length of her body as she dropped her head or moved her arm or did the thing that made that metal on concrete sound of cans moving. He was startled until he realized he was at the top of the stoop, right next to the door that led to the hallway, that led to the door that led to the kitchen that led to his mama sticking her head out the window making sure everything was still alright, glancing out the window to see her baby sitting, but staring at the street moving closer, opening its eyes to see the child staring at the times moving closer, the anger moving closer, the fuckyoumotherfuckers being tossed through the air and into ears, hands, lips, nose, eyes staring but sitting at the top of the stoop trying to dream as Mama screams, "Boy, get your ass in here," as he closes his eyes and wonders for the first time if dreams had to be like this.

The First Few Minutes

They slap my baby. The baby starts to breathe, so I don't smoke that crack today. I stay home, listen to the news, and start getting nervous. Baby squeezes my finger. Baby smiles, so I don't give a dollar to that nigger on my street. I keep that dollar and buy a dozen eggs. I keep that dollar and think about the future.

Baby calls me daddy or da da or something, so I stop fucking around. I start shaving on a regular basis and put that hole in that peg like I'm told.

Baby's crawling around today, so I go ahead and get that house. I go ahead and ask for that promotion. I go ahead and kiss that ass.

Baby's taking steps now, so I start thinking about my baby living forever. I want all those niggers behind bars. I want more cops in my neighborhood. I want bigger, better jails. I want more justice.

Baby wants to sleep outside, so I want the outside cleaned up right. No sex, no drugs, no dirty words, just God, and love, and pretty birds. Just Quayles and Bush and PTL and talk of heaven, never hell, and talk of heaven, never hell, but they slap my baby, my baby starts to breathe.

THE SIN

She is on her knees. Mama wants forgiveness for her sins. I see her begging. Begging to God for mercy, begging to God for time. Begging to God for something more than life.

She is on her knees, and I'm angered by the scars the ground has made. I'm angered by her closed eyes. I'm angered by her faith, by her humility.

She is on her knees and I want her to stand. I want to take her hands and make her stand. I want to take her hands and make her see. I want to slap her back to me, but she is on her knees.

I must fall to my knees to lift her, and when I'm on my knees, she holds me there. She embraces me. I become aware of her sins, and she forgives me.

To the Rocks for Mama

The phone rings 3 a.m. tears from melodies of unresistable heartbeats breathing in song, breathing in anger, in Mama's tears. His mama cries, "One of my babies is dead. One of my babies been killed. He was a good boy." She sings through 3 a.m. tears awakening. She sings, "My baby was a good boy." And the phone is gripped tighter as the melody bewitches her children with pulse, with the music of her 3 a.m. call. And her voice is a siren. She is the singer of songs made alive in her call, granting birth to desperate anger and tears awakening, calling her babies to Scylla and Charybdis, to Avalon and Century, to the rocks, to the rocks, through the silence, through the dial tone, her voice is a siren singing, a siren alive.

Alive, her baby cries. His brother cries. His brother cries. He hears his siren's song. Mama's crying and he hears his siren singing loss, singing anger, singing his destination, Avalon & Century, Scylla & Charybdis, the rocks, the rocks where his brother awaits, where tears await. The phone rings 3 a.m. tears from melodies of unresistable heartbeats breathing in song, breathing in Mama's crying, in Mama's tears.

"Mama wants a good boy," she sings, "Mama wants another good boy." But the phone keeps ringing. Her tears have drowned them all.

"Your father did that to her?"

"Yeah."

"He must've been a pig."

"Yeah, I guess."

"You guess? Well, let me be the first to tell you, your father was a pig."

"Well, he said she stole his soul."

"Oh, so your father was full of shit too?"

"I guess."

"You guess? He beat your mother to within an inch of her life. I don't need to know anymore."

"Yeah, well, he came home drunk that night, and she split his skull with a cast-iron skillet."

"So that didn't give him the right to do what he did to her. Your father's a pig."

"Hey, if you ain't gonna listen, you better stop talking about my father like that."

"Or what? You're gonna do to me what your father did to her?"

"No. My father was wrong, but my mother was just as wrong as he was. I don't think I want to be like either of them. They both went too far and they never came back. Then she hit him, he fell down hard, and she didn't even try to help him, so he just kept falling. He was drunk, but that just made him bleed more. There was so much blood on the floor around his head. Later on, what he told me seemed like the truth. It looked like there was a halo growing in a red stream from his skull, and maybe it was his soul, cause no one could've bled that much, and he wasn't even unconscious. He didn't even seem weak. As a matter of fact, he kept hitting the ground, he kept hitting the floor harder than I'd seen him hit anything, but at the same time, he looked like he was dying. He was looking in her eyes, she had to see, but she was just screaming at him, "Yeah, motherfucker.

Yeah, motherfucker. You better not ever come into my house like that." She was screaming and screaming, and his head was on the floor and his halo was growing, and he was dying, but when she finished yelling, she didn't offer her hand. She went to their room, slammed the door, and locked it. My father's eyes followed her until the door blocked his vision, and he spotted me standing in the opened doorway to my bedroom. I couldn't hide. I couldn't pretend to be asleep. His face was wet with blood, but I knew he was crying. He stared at me for a very long moment, then the halo stopped growing. He got up, broke through the door that led to my mother, I heard him hit her, and I heard her landing on the closet mirror."

"That pig. That pig. That motherfucking pig. What did you do? Just stand there?"

"When I heard him hit her, I ran to their room. She was on the floor, unconscious. I knew I had to get to her, but his eyes froze me at the door. They never left me as he picked up the phone, dialed, all I heard him say was "Help." His entire body was drenched in a night tinted, purplish red, Well, everything but his eyes. They seemed so white there had to be nothing inside."

"What about your mother?"

"I ran to her and she was twisted where she'd fallen. I tried to move her away from that broken mirror, but I was only six, and she was too heavy. I returned my father's glance, begging him for help but "She stole my soul, boy. She took everything," was all he said. I looked up, and the police were in the room. And as the ambulance took me and my mother away, I saw my father being handcuffed and led to a squad car."

"Yeah, I hope he rotted in jail."

"Yeah, her injuries were so severe that he got two years."

"That's all?"

"Yeah, I guess, but we never saw him again."

THE ONE WHO REALLY LOVES HER

I caught him in front of a bar on 83rd and Halsted. Somebody was tossing his drunk ass out on the street. He was trying to say, "Fuck you" or something like that, but it was coming out like you'd expect from a drunk ass motherfucker slipping over syllables. He landed face first on the concrete, too drunk to move his hands fast enough to stop the sidewalk, and the sidewalk opened his face. He was already bleeding peppermint schnapps when I hit him the first time.

"Yeah, motherfucker. Yeah, motherfucker. You ain't so bad now," I said as I yanked that nine-inch-nailed baseball bat from his stomach, cocked it and prepared to swing it again. His heart was pumping alcohol and he needed to fall down somewhere, but when he recognized me, he knew he had to summon up a little more time.

"I love your mama, boy," he moaned spitting blood from his concrete ripped lower lip. "I love your mama," he said as I swung and the nail entered the hands protecting his head from me and my anger.

"She loves me. She loves me," he cried as I remembered her face only fifteen minutes ago, a swollen piece of misshapen pulp with only a whisper of beaten flesh preventing bruises and cuts from opening to wash my mother's beauty down to the place I was gonna take this motherfucker when I made first contact, when I made all contact necessary to open up his skull.

"She loves me," he said and I swung that bat.

"She loves me," he said and I swung to kill, fully aware of the crowd coming from the bar, from the streets, from my neighborhood, circling me and that nigger as I swung to tear his hands away from his head, to expose his drunken red eyes, to touch the spot that would end his love for my mother forever.

"She loves me," echoes in my head, and I could feel that crowd circling, closing, eyes transfixed to witness the silence I had every intention of providing as I continued to puncture the hands hiding him, hiding silence, hiding that spot.

"She loves me," he whispered, crying.

"Shut up, motherfucker," I screamed as I could feel his drunk ass finally giving up.

"Shut up, motherfucker," I said as his arms dropped, and his bleeding red eyes stared begging to the son he'd lost with the drunken swing of fists upon flesh and blood, upon mothers and sons, upon love, love.

"She loves me," he said, as I took that bat and raised it above my head, but "I love him" echoed from her lips as I left her 15 minutes ago to find a way to make him stop.

"I don't know what to say to you, boy," he said stepping down on the accelerator and pulling away from the house he used to live in, the house he was still paying for but had to knock on the door to get into these days.

"I don't know how to fill this time," he said, keeping his eyes on the road, careful not to look down and to his right, to the boy sitting on the seat beside him buckled up nice and tight playing some video game, carefully. Carefully, so he didn't have to look up and to his left. The sound of the game was turned up high, so he didn't have to hear his father telling him, "This is not enough for me. They won't let me have enough time to tell you what I know, to show you what I've seen, what I've done."

The boy pressed buttons quickly, trying not to pay attention as his father turned onto the expressway and pushed the pedal down wondering how far he could travel in this allotted time, how long could he travel before the boy's mother called the cops, how far could he go on 76 dollars and forty-nine cents. Could he tell his boy a lifetime in that time? Could he tell him what he thought he needed to know?

"I love you, son," he said, but the words didn't feel like enough, so he pushed down on the accelerator, and they were suddenly moving ninety miles an hour. His son lost interest in the video game, as the car picked up speed and he arched his back to see over the dashboard as his father slipped fluidly through cars that appeared to be standing still as they flew down the expressway. Every part of the boy's body was alive and listening when his father said, "Life is short." Then touched the pedal the last quarter of an inch to the floor, "Live it before they take it away."

He couldn't think of anything else to say so he called the boy's name and when his head turned he turned away from the road to look directly in the eyes for a moment stretched to an eternity moving at 110 miles an hour. He looked into his child's eyes stretching that moment for what need to be a lifetime of avoiding disasters coming too fast, avoiding disasters on instinct and intuition and moving as fluid through oncoming traffic without turning away from his boy, without turning away from his boy for this moment.

But when the boy turned away to see the cars coming and going too fast, he felt the car slowing down. In a moment, they were stopped at a gas station on the side of the road. It took a couple seconds for the boy to take his eyes away from the windshield. The world was still moving to him even though the ground and the car had stopped.

He glanced over to his father whose eyes were closed. With his eyes closed, he placed the keys into his boy's hands, stepped out of the car and walked away, down the expressway, thumbing for a ride. The boy put the keys in his pocket and slid over to the driver's seat. His feet couldn't reach the pedals, but if he stood up, he could see what was coming and what was going too fast. As the cars passed by his father walking away, he steered the wheels left and right in a car he was too young to move, and as his father vanished down the expressway, he watched the cars flying by as he stood still, looking for, waiting for enough time.

THE PILOT STANDS ON HENNEPIN
FOR JUMA

He had to reach above his head to touch the end of the wall. He was five years old, but with a little effort he lifted his body, and soon he was standing one hundred feet tall, gazing down upon floor after floor, window after window, then suddenly, sidewalk, street, alley, and man. There were clouds above him, but his eyes focused on his father vanishing into eye-level horizon. He stood at the end of the wall, watching until there was nothing to see. He stood one hundred feet tall, eyes unblinking, hoping he was tall enough, hoping this time his father would look back and see him, look back and see a man he could not fall. He wanted his father to look back and see a man in the clouds with him.

Belts, Fists, Tazers, Clubs, Pistols, Teargas, Prisons and the Making of a Law-Abiding Citizen

It was time to whip my baby's ass, so I got the belt from my closet, wrapped it around my hand, and found a reason. When he saw me, he tried to run to his mama, but I caught him. I detained him. It was time to whip his ass. Somebody out there said it was time to whip his ass, so I was gonna whip his ass, so he knew and would know when this time came again.

"Get on your knees." "Put your hands above your head, boy." "Don't you fight." Don't you fight now, boy. It's time. It's time they said, and I snapped my belt across his ass until I heard the tears coming loud and he had no choice but to try and run, but when he ran, I hit him harder, when he ran, I whipped him longer. It was time to whip my baby's ass. Somebody out there said it was time to whip my baby's ass so he knew and would know when this time came again.

"Shut up, boy," was all I said. "Shut up, boy," was all I said, but I knew I had something more to say. I knew I should have been talking him through it like his mama does, but his mama don't get beat on the street like that. His mama might get the benefit of a rod or two before the clubs came out. Somebody might read his mama her rights, but I had no words. I didn't know why. Somebody on the TV said, somebody on the radio said, somebody outside my window said it was time to whip my baby's ass, so I was gonna whip his ass, so he knew and would know when this time came again.

I was making calluses for when that time came again. You see, somebody said an ass should be beat for that. I've been beaten for that. Niggers get beat for that. I had to save my boy. Niggers can die for that.

The Momentary Life and Sudden Death of a Mad Dog

I was as deeply asleep as a caseload of forty ounces can get you until I heard them down the hallway, and I opened my eyes. For a second, I didn't know where I was, or what the fuck I was hearing. Then I saw them through a half-opened door in an unlit room. She was saying, singing, "It's gonna be alright, baby, don't be afraid." Cradling our child in one arm and wiping its tears with the other, her voice was saying, singing the words into a constitutional certainty, "It's alright, baby, it's alright."

It was dark where I was, but there was enough moon to light the apartment and show me where I had to go. I stood up but tripped over the cord to the broken lamp still wrapped around my ankle. The cord that put me down and to sleep on the floor I just woke up from. I took the cord from my ankle and got up again. My baby was crying. My lady was saving my baby, and I had to make myself a part of this. Daddy was coming. Daddy was gonna save the day, but I took a step and smashed my foot against the TV set I could just barely remember throwing against the wall earlier that night. I fell and cut my arm on a piece of that shattered picture tube.

"Goddamit," I shouted, and I could hear the pitch of my baby's tears change and grow a little louder now, but my lady's words, her song stayed a constant melody.

"Don't be afraid," she said. "Don't be afraid." I tried to lift myself up by pressing my hands against the floor, but there was a pain in my knuckles. I glanced down and they were swelled to double size. They were stained with a red I thought was blood at first, but on closer observation, I realized my hands were uncut, and I was looking at a lipstick smear in the shape of my lady's mouth.

"Don't be afraid," she said as my baby's tears fell louder, and I stood opening eyes blurred and suddenly terrified by the path leading to my family, there was a hole punched into the hallway wall in the shape of a fist, a phone ripped from its socket and in pieces, I remember making blood drops on the floor, red hands above the doorknob.

"It's alright," she said, mellifluous in tone as I continued staggering down the hallway to deliver my salvation, to heal all wounds, to end my baby's tears and make everything alright. "Don't be afraid. Don't be afraid," she said as I opened the door, and my baby screamed at the sight of me, of my return.

"Don't be afraid," slid mellifluously from her lips as I entered the room and dropped to my knees pleading, but knowing I could never be forgiven for these sins. My baby was twisted and bruised with tears that recognized me and fell in horror. My hands and fist had been there, and I realized I could never touch my child gently again, that my hand extended would always bring a twinge of fear, that my hand extended had once been and would always be a fist to my child. I closed my eyes, but a vivid picture of the evening's sins forced them open again.

"It's gonna be alright," flowed from deep inside of my lady. My baby's arms wrapped around her tightly and freed the hand that grabbed the pistol. I smiled when she pointed it at my face. Still on my knees, I extended my arms. It was my offer of salvation. When I could no longer hear her song, I knew she had made everything alright just like she said she would.

PICTURE OF THE MAN

When she burned his pictures, he grew. He became ten feet tall, a mile wide, and as powerful, as relentless as the ocean flow. He became more than a man. He became what I dreamed him to be, and as his posed smile melted, bubbled, and chipped away, broken by fire, broken by mystery, broken by her hands, I inhaled that fire and spit it in her direction. When she burned his pictures, she said goodbye to him, but my eyes ignited when she tossed her match, and for thirty seconds of fire, each blink became a flashbulbed fantasy. A nigger burned to man, a man burned to hero, a hero burned to god. She tossed her match, flash! I burned into a picture of him.

"It's alright," he said. His children were sitting on the front stoop playing something that involved a lot of screaming. He'd caught them in the corner of his eyes and walked over for a better look.

"It's alright," he thought, smiling slowly. A tickle ran up his spine.

"It's alright," he whispered, careful not to move the curtain, careful not to be seen, carefully keeping the moment alive. He just wanted to see that moment. He just wanted to see what he'd done and inhale, inhale that moment for as long as it lasted. He stood beside the window, daydreaming as that moment became thick in his lungs.

"It's alright," he said. "It's alright." But his hands were trembling and he'd never been so afraid in his life.

His First Steps

She don't hit him anymore, not since his fingers grew into the palm of his hand. "Get your ass over here, boy." Smack! "Sit your ass down, boy." Smack! "Do you hear me, boy?" Smack! Smack! Smack don't happen anymore. She don't hit anymore, not since he bent those baby fingers tight and pushed those knuckles out, not since he started swinging eight-year-old arms that ended in fists, not since he started making contact during asswhippings, not since he hit her. The world got as black as her womb again when he hit her. Her fists opened to fingers and palm protecting scars, protecting her three times broken nose, her countlessly blackened eyes, her busted, misshapen lips. Her fist opened to cover places beaten by all those previous niggers, and she don't hit him anymore. She don't hit him anymore. Where her baby used to stand, she sees another nigger. She looks in his eyes, she sees a bitch reflecting. Mama ain't mama no more. Baby ain't baby, and she don't hit him anymore. She don't hit him anymore. She don't hold him anymore. She don't love him anymore. His fist is cocked. He could hit her. His dick is hard. He's gonna hit her. A nigger is born. Her child has died in his fists, but he's eight years old. She could find her leather strap and whip his black ass. He's eight years old. Her fist is bigger. She could beat his motherfucking ass. He's eight years old. She could kill that nigger. She could kill that nigger now. She could kill that nigger now, but she don't hit him anymore. She won't hit him anymore.

"Ain't no such thing as children anymore." That's what I told them when they knocked on my door that night.

"He just came out that way." That's what I said, and they agreed. "Ain't no such thing as children anymore. Ain't no such thing as children anymore."

He was a man when I prayed for cum strong enough to create him. He was a man when I stuck my dick, naked, into his mama. He was a man when he emerged from her legs to see a black dick hanging. He ain't never been a child. He ain't never been a child. There was only birth and manhood for that nigger, birth and manhood, and ain't no such thing as children anymore.

"Ain't no such thing as children anymore." No helplessness, no ignorance, no innocence, no children, no children, no such thing as children, there ain't no such thing as children, just men, just men and him, just men and worthless motherfuckers like him. And they agreed, and they agreed, "Ain't no such thing as children anymore. Ain't no such thing as children anymore."

And then they told me about how he was a suspect, about how they had to use their guns to restrain him, about how he almost got away but they found him (like they always do) sucking on his mama's breast or crying for someone, anyone to please take the shit away, please take the shit away. They asked me if I had a pair of Huggies for that nigger. They asked me to shut his motherfucking ass up for them, so I went to his bedroom, stepped over the Care Bear blanket and dinosaur rattle, ducked by the Old McDonald mobiles, and opened his closet. There was seventeen years worth of Huggies he was never gonna need, ain't no such thing as children anymore, so I gave them all the Huggies in the closet. I even tossed in his favorite pacifier. When they left, I went to his room, ignoring the odor of helplessness, of ignorance, ignoring the odor of Johnson's baby powder and Gerber applesauce-induced shit on my fingers. I ignored the six pounds and three ounces of life released from my arms.

"Ain't no such thing as children anymore. Ain't no such thing as children anymore. He was a man. He was a man," I said. I smelled my fingers. I weighed my arms. But "Ain't no such thing as children anymore. He was a man," I said.

WALKING THROUGH A GRAVEYARD AT THE AGE OF EIGHT

He was scared, and his mama said, "Don't be scared." So he's been standing like a man all this time.

He was scared, and his mama said, "Don't be scared," but he was screaming through his hand placed trembling to his mouth. He was screaming as the children played with fists and guns on the blood soaked concrete of the park behind the school, screaming through the alley behind the liquor store behind his home, the alley filled with cum shot rubbers, broken basepipes, and niggers with dead hearts beating.

The air he breathed was thick with fear. His hand was on his mouth. He was scared. And his mama said, "Don't be scared." But there were sounds seeping through his fingers when the night fell to rape the children, the city lacked all means of escape, and the fires burned. He was scared, and his mama said, "Don't be scared," but his hands weren't enough to stop the screams. His hands were too small to hold back the fear, so he learned to stand like a man in the fear. He learned to raise his fist in the fear, so there was nothing in the fear, nothing in the fear.

He was scared, and his mama said, "Don't be scared." So his eyes are yes are black now. His sky is black now. His world is black now. There is nothing in the fear. There is nothing to fear. He was scared, and his mama said, "Don't be scared," so he walks in nothing, standing, and he questions his mama's tears.

ALL I NEEDED TO KNOW
FOR RONALD BENJAMIN JONES

I never expected to meet him. I was almost thirty when I got his phone call. "This is your father. If you want to meet me, I'm at Max's on 94th Street. You'll know me." And he hung up the phone. I got dressed and went over there. Max's was about ten blocks, so I walked. My mother had no pictures of him, so I had no idea what he looked like. But I'd dreamed of a thousand faces in my lifetime, and I reviewed every one on that walk.

When I opened the door, there were four men at the bar, two empty booths, two with couples, and a man at the end of the room, standing, staring at the door, staring at my face. When I looked into his eyes, he crossed the room, and I prepared the thousand questions I thought I had to ask. I prepared the thousand answers I thought he would need. I prepared myself for denials, frustrations, anger. And as he moved closer, I made a fist. As he moved closer, I extended my arms. As he moved closer, I walked away but stood still. He crossed the room and took my hand. He pulled me close and whispered in my ear. "Now we know, now we know," he said. And walked out the door.

I bought a beer and stared at the mirror behind the bar. I never saw my father again, but when I looked in that mirror, I knew him. When I looked in that mirror, I'd known him all my life. When I looked in that mirror, into my eyes, I knew he'd be there soon.

LEARNING TO USE MY VEINS

Inside Out Alive with Pipe

The curtain's closed. He peeks through the cracks. He feels it on his fingertips. He wants to lick them dry, but he's shaking. They're coming this time.

"Hide," he whispers. "Run." Or if I stand here against this wall they'll miss me. They'll miss me, maybe. No, this time they'll see. This time they're here. This time, this time. This time he's in the closet. The light off. The light bulb removed. He's invisible.

"I'm invisible," he thinks on his knees picking at the prayed white chip of nothing he thought he saw on the floor, that time when he was gonna give this shit up and he had the strength to throw that rock in the corner, and it must've broke apart or something cause there's something on this floor somewhere.

And if I check every little speck of nothing, there's gonna be something, somewhere. So I better get my pipe out my pocket, cause it's around here somewhere. But... he freezes. Something's looking. It's cold and makes him naked, obvious. It's peeking through the cracks. They're peeking through the cracks, and he's in the center of the floor, obvious. The curtain's closed. "They're coming." It's here. The curtain's closed. The crack peeks through.

DELICACIES

He shit his pants for the first time in years tonight. The fall was finally over. The fall was complete. He slipped from his feet to his knees to the ground, and he didn't want to get up anymore. He shit his pants and he didn't feel a desperate need for toilet paper anymore. He didn't worry about the stain that shit was gonna make anymore. The smell of shit didn't hurt his nose anymore, and he shit his pants for the first time in years tonight.

It wasn't the locked toilet at the corner gas station. It wasn't the fear of a bug crawling up his ass while squatting in the bushes. It wasn't the public spectacle of himself if he shit on the sidewalk. He just had to shit, so he shit his pants. He shit his pants for the first time in years tonight. He let it soak through the air around him. He let it soak through, so the people walking by would know.

And he cried, and he cried, and he cried until everybody knew, until nobody gave a fuck anymore. He cried until he was a child alone, until he was a baby, until all he could do was wait for his man and say, "It's alright, baby. Everything's gonna be alright." He shit his pants, but Mama's gonna make it better. Mama's gonna wipe his ass. Mama's gonna hear his tears. Mama's gonna take him home for the first time in years, tonight.

Mama's Little Bad Boy
for Paula and Kenny

She never hit her baby, not unless he was bad.

He'd had his ass whipped a couple times, but only when he was being bad. He wasn't being bad. She could think well enough to know he wasn't being bad. Holding her wasn't being bad, but she hadn't had a hit in a couple of days and the check arrived. The check was cashed, the check was a rock unwrapped and waiting in her fingertips as he held her. She had her pipe out. She wanted her rock to burn on that pipe. She wanted to get high, but he was holding her. He wasn't being bad. He was holding her. That wasn't being bad at the moment. That wasn't being bad at the moment. She was being bad at the moment. He wrapped his arm around her, tried to lay his head on her chest, pull her closer, but she wanted to get away. She wanted to break his grip and get high. She hadn't had a hit in a couple of days, and she wanted to get high. She needed to get high, but he was not letting her go. He was demanding his mother. He was holding on.

She never hit her baby, not unless he was bad. But she hadn't had a hit in a couple of days, and that itch in the back of her brain was holding her too, demanding she get high. She had to get high, and he was holding her, and holding her was bad at the moment, holding her was bad at the moment.

She never hit her baby, not unless he was bad, but she had to scratch that itch. She had to pull him off of her and light the rock in her fingers, but he was holding on. She told him to go play, so she could scratch that itch for the length of a rock on fire, but his arms around her were bad. She told him to get the fuck away from her, so she could get the fuck away, but he was not letting her go. He was holding her. He was being bad. He was being bad.

She never hit her baby, not unless he was bad, but he was holding his mother. He was being bad. He was demanding his mother. He was being bad. His mother was abused. His mother was beaten. His mother was leaving him a little more every time she took a hit. His mother was leaving him every time she got high. His mother was leaving him, so he was holding her. He was holding her tightly. He was being bad. He was being bad.

She never hit her baby, not unless he was bad, but holding her was bad at the moment, so she made a fist. She made a fist with her unwrapped rock singing a siren's song to the hungry veins leading to the back of her brain. She made a fist needing that slick smoke flow to slide through her burned glass pipe and re-educate her unslapped brain on the intricacies of love and flight. She made a fist, and she was gonna get high, goddamnit. That rock and that pipe were gonna teach her how to escape his grip with her fist. Her fist was gonna get her high.

She never hit her baby, not unless he was bad, but his arms were around her, and she made a fist. She made a fist curling white-knuckled fingers into her palm tightly, tightly. She made a fist so tight, too tight, too tight to hold the glass pipe in her hand. Snap! She broke the glass pipe in her hand and her fist released itself into an arm. Her fist became an arm, an arm wrapping trembling fist around him, an arm embracing, an arm embracing. She held her baby in her arms. She held her baby with a white-knuckled fist bleeding on embracing arms, with a white-knuckled fist fighting to hold her baby, fighting to remind her. She could never hit her baby, not unless he was bad.

She could never hit her baby, not unless he was bad, so she had to hold her baby tightly. She had to hold her baby with fingernails digging deeply into the bleeding palm of a white-knuckled fist. She had to hold her baby.

She never hit her baby, not unless he was bad, so she would hold him tightly. She would hold him until she could pull him away, until he went outside to play, until he stopped holding her. He was good. He was good. She would hold him until he was bad. She would hold him until he was bad. She would hold him until he was bad and he let her go, but he wrapped his arms around her. He held his mother tightly, staring at the broken glass bleeding in her hands and at her feet. He held her tighter and tighter. He knew he would have to hold her forever. He held her forever.

DROPPED, FALLEN, SHATTERED

They lived three buildings from the corner, and he would watch her as she stood there in her tube top and her spandex biker pants lighting cigarettes to set her aside from the night and attract the drivers passing. He would stare until she was a blur of colors, and he didn't see a woman anymore, until she wasn't a living thing anymore, until she was just the thing that was gonna bring these drugs home, a thing unaware of the pain, the humiliation, the ten-dick-a-night degradation blurring his vision of her, blurring his vision, until he didn't see a woman anymore, until he just saw a thing to be made useless, a thing to be fucked, a thing to be beaten, a thing to fill his pipe every night without fail as long as he kept her alive, and as long as he didn't see too clearly, as long as he didn't see a woman, his woman, not a woman, not anymore.

He would stare out the window as she stood there, and he would try to forget the places he'd touched her, the places he'd touched when she was a friend, when she was a lover, when she was something that could have been touched forever, until forever lit a pipe, took a hit and became the time it takes to get that next hit, and became the time it takes to get that next hit. He stared out the window at the blur on the corner forgetting the urge to touch her.

"Forever needs a hit," he'd say. A car stops beside her. She guides it around the corner, and he has to move to another window to see her. She sticks her head into the passenger window, her blue spandex ass twitching to the driver's twenty dollar offer. She enters the car and moves down the alley to the back door. He is hiding on the bathroom floor when she fucks on the living room couch. He is hiding in the hallway closet when she fucks in the kitchen. He is hiding outside when she fucks in the bedroom. He is hiding. He is hiding. He is hiding when those twenty dollar bills ignite his pipe and he dreams of touching her again, and he dreams of touching her forever.

THE NIGGER KISSES WINGS

I close my eyes. I am high. I am flying, a snakelike black liquid slithering down Halsted Avenue, elevated by the smack in my bloodstream, the silence rising, lifting the wings attaching my arms to the skin ripped away from the callused and alley-stained back I'm sleeping on.

I am flying with flesh-coated wings that create the possibility of flight, the possibility of flight for a moment between falls, but I am falling now, rising above the piss I'm leaving in the hallway, the bullet-holed flesh I'm breathing through, and my eyes without hope pinched naked with desire, a desire to fly. I extend my arms, unfurl my wings, and I can see my blood inside. It is crying. It is spilling. I am falling.

I open my eyes. She is asleep. It's dark. It's late, but I can see the room immediately. We are sleeping on a mattress. The only other piece of furniture is a dresser in the corner. Her purse is on top of it. A check for $156.00 is inside that purse. We have been together for a month since my time on the street. I have made promises. Our child is asleep in the room beside us. I have made promises. I want to hold them for the rest of my life, but I stand up. I walk to her purse. There is a mirror standing above the dresser. It looks me in the eyes. I tear through her bag to find the check, and I'm staring at me. I'm staring at me as I can feel my wings growing, ripping loose from my back. My lady awakens to my hand in her purse. Our child wanders into the room, and the mirror is staring hard. I am staring hard as I scream, "Don't you want to see me fly?"

I extend my arms.

"Don't you want to see me fly?" I say.

DOWN

A dream ended. Something was said, but I didn't hear. That something woke me up, but I was too tired to get up, so I just laid there with my eyes closed. I didn't want to go to sleep again. I just laid there, waiting.

"Boy! I told you to get up," she said, "now get your black ass up!" I heard Mama walking down the hallway to the front door. There was a slam, and she was gone. I stayed in bed, my eyes closed, awake. At first, I was just breathing. Then I could smell the air. Monday's aroma was sticking to the walls, so I took a deep breath, dozed off for what seemed like a minute but when I opened my eyes it was 10:49. Mama left at 7:00 everyday. School started at eight, and this Tuesday I was gonna be late again.

The curtains were drawn, and even though the sun was up, it was still dark in my room so I moved slowly. I was dressed but I felt dirty. I'd slept in my clothes. I got up, pulled on a shirt, some draws, and some pants from the closet. It was the first time I'd moved since Bruce left the night before. I tossed the old clothes, got dressed, opened the curtain, and it was finally Tuesday. It was time to recover. Monday was party night for me and Bruce. We had a good contact and would get first shot at the best shit in the city every Monday, and every Monday we'd get together, get a couple of ladies, and party till fucked, out of shit, or Mama came home.

Mondays were perfect. We got 'inside' on Mondays. That's what we like to call it, getting 'inside', getting into a dream, going up instead of falling down. Getting 'inside' on Mondays made the 'outside' cool for the rest of the week. It was enough to make everything cool.

I fucked. Bruce fucked, and when the girls left last night, we both should have been smiling. I was smiling, but as we rolled that last bit of shit into a joint, he wasn't smiling. I lay on my bed. He sat with his back against the wall, within arm's length. He lit the joint, took a long and desperate hit, then passed it to me.

In silence. We passed it back and forth silently for a while. About halfway through, he started talking. I wasn't listening at first, but when I looked over to get the joint, I saw his face. It was tired and hungry.

"I can't dream anymore," he said. "I don't know how to dream." He took another desperate hit from the joint. "This shit won't let me dream anymore."

He took that hit like he was starving and I'd seen that need before. I'd seen that need outside. It was Monday and he was bringing the outside in here, so I stared at the ceiling. He was my closest friend, more than a brother could be, but he was too damned tired, and he was bringing the outside in on my Monday. He was fucking up my high. I stared at the ceiling, snatched the joint, took a quick hit, a proper hit and passed it back, silently. I wanted the talk to stop. I was seeing things more clearly, and I wanted him to stop talking. I was starting to think of the falling and the fallen, and I wanted to stay high. He was talking about the 'outside' when he was as close to 'inside' as we were ever gonna get. We were 'inside' and he was fucking up my high. I was gonna tell him he was fucking up my high until I saw that tear. When I turned away from the ceiling to take the joint, I saw it rolling down the side of his cheek, falling. He was falling, and it should have been time to wake up. It was time to watch his back. It was time to get strong, but it was time to get high. It was time to be 'inside'. He handed me the joint in silence. When I took it the tear had vanished and it was as if it had never fallen. He looked as high as me. He closed his eyes and smiled as he took the joint and sucked it away. We were back 'inside' there would be no more tears that night, and then he was gone.

It was 11 a.m. I was one late motherfucker. I tried to breathe a little Monday off the curtain, but it was gone. I glanced out the window, and there were lights flashing. Cops, I thought, who they fucking with now? I took a better look downstairs and they were attached to an ambulance. Who died? I leaned over a little more, but I was too high up to see, so I gave up and headed for the door. Bruce didn't come up and get me, so I figured he was still downstairs waiting for me.

I locked my door and looked down the hall to the elevator. I saw someone sitting on the window, still looking downstairs at the flashing lights. I thought it was Bruce but it was the girl I fucked last night. She was staring, focusing downstairs as if there was too much action down there to turn away from. When I got to the elevator, she still hadn't moved, not even to breathe it seemed, but when I got closer, things got clear. Next to her, on the sill was a syringe and a rubber hose. I'd known her all her life, and she'd been using for a while now. She wasn't really staring out the window. She was just inhaling in her own special way.

When I pushed the elevator button she woke up, angry until she recognized me, then cool, "What's happening?" she said. "What hap, babe?" The lights by the elevator were blown out, and there were bars on the windows, so it was kind of dark. I moved slowly, so did she. I kept my eyes on her. I knew what she would do for a dollar, what she would do to stay high. Staying high was much too important to her for me to look away, so I kept my eyes open. She was in the shadows, where I couldn't see her face, where only her frame was visible, covered by a fallen sheet of black granted by the shadow of the elevator. Her head bobbed as if she were trying to go to sleep but couldn't wake up. She looked at me again, as if she'd forgotten I was there.

"I just got some stuff from out of state," she paused, expecting my interest to rise. When it didn't, she continued. "You give me ten dollars and we keep your party going all night tonight too." But it was Tuesday and her shit was for everyday, so I went through my pocket, overlooked a twenty. "I'm tapped out," I said, then changed the subject, looked downstairs. "Who died?" I said.

"Who cares?" she said. The elevator doors opened. I got in, pushed the down button. The doors closed, and she was gone. Bruce lived on the first floor. I went down. The lower I got, the more talk I heard. When I reached the first floor, the doors opened, and sound released itself into the elevator. There was too much talk to hear anything, but I could see the paramedics wheeling a covered body out the door. There was none of that resuscitation shit going on, so the body was gone. I was too fucking late to be curious, so I headed over to Bruce's apartment. Where he would be waiting. Where he should have been waiting, but as they pushed the body past, I knew he wasn't waiting. I could smell Monday under that covering sheet, and I knew he wasn't waiting anymore. I followed the crowd outside. I followed the crowd outside and I could see them loading him into the back of that ambulance. He was covered by a sheet, but as they passed him into the shadow of that ambulance, I knew what was inside. I looked inside, and I could see his face again. He was 'inside' again, as if a tear had never fallen. I closed my eyes, sniffed my hands searching for any small bit of Monday's aroma on my fingertips, but it was too late. It was Tuesday, and I was too late, but I had to get inside again. I walked through the crowd to the elevator. I got in, pushed the button. I was outside. It was Tuesday, but I needed more. And as the elevator doors closed and as the sound of the outside was pushed away as I rose, the shadow on my hallway window sill became clear, and I knew she would bring me 'inside.' She would bring me inside today or everyday. She would bring me 'inside' everyday and tell me what to want, tell us both what to want. I smelled the air, Monday was coming, Monday was coming again.

THE MYTH OF INVISIBILITY

I am invisible crawling deeper into this alley until I light the pipe and step away from the night, until I appear in a flash glowing through cracked dreams and inhalations of blinked caresses separating me from my invisibility, from my cocaine dwindling, burning to the last hit. I take that last hit, and the alley is dark, the alley is black until he enters. All other light trickling down upon me originates from that seventy story world above me, a safe distance away from me, downtown. I light the pipe. The Bic flame reveals me as I take the last hit and he walks past, his twenty-five to forty years of perfect clean stepping effortlessly over the piss stains falling from the garbage cans, his twenty-five to forty years of perfect clean calling me nigger with a Rolex watch, a Giorgio Armani suit, and hands unstained, unscarred, untouched, his perfect clean alive and flaunting it, bringing clean alive and flaunting it, bringing light from seventy stories away while I stand invisible.

I am invisible as I stop him. "Don't you know who I am, motherfucker? Don't you know who I am?" I say, a vision crawling from the alley to stand hidden by the dark but closing the alley between seventy story stars and the motherfucker at my fingertips finally realizing the world is on fire in his black back alley and one of us, only one of us, has the light on.

THE LAST PLACE ON EARTH

He found a seat at the end of the bar, ordered a Jack Daniel's, and looked around for a spot to stare at for the evening. He'd been drinking at this place for about two years now, and he was running out of new spots to occupy his eyes, but he didn't feel like finding someplace else to go, so he tried not to give a fuck about the detached familiarity, and settled in. He just wanted to sit. He just wanted to listen to any different noise that might occur, any different voice, any different nothing. He just wanted to get lost. He just wanted to get a little bit lost for a while, to be a shadow at the end of the bar, unnoticed, unnoticeable, a heartbeat sipping on a Jack Daniel's for as long as is necessary to disappear.

The bartender still didn't know his name, but even after two years of three word sentences, she was always polite, so he spared her an eternity of weekly sob stories and left that to every other fool in the bar, and he would listen with varying degrees of interest as she would pull each different nightmare from their slightly inebriated lips, as she would caress their dreams and massage the edges with Wild Turkey, schnapps, and Absolut absolutes.

"How you doin' tonight?" she said, slipping him the Jack Daniel's. He nodded, handing her the three bucks to include the tip. She nodded a thank you and in a moment she was at the end of the bar exposing wisdom and keeping her ears open for slurred syllables, spilled drinks, and words heated by tequila. When she was that far away, she might as well have been on the other end of the world. When there was nothing to listen to, he tended to get lost inside a chosen spot on the wall, and the conversation was happening about twenty feet away, so he was going inside. He lit a cigarette and took the first drag without losing that spot. His eyes were carefully positioned behind the third table on the left, about two feet above. He was staring at the autographed picture of Paul Chambers picking at the strings of an upright bass with sweat staining his dark two piece suit and a thin tie perfect with the small exception of a five o'clock turn just before the end. As he stared at the picture, he could hear Davis and Coltrane sliding in and out of the strings of that bass, stirring his heartbeat and tipping his glass until he was about two sips away from needing another Jack's.

He put the glass down, tapped his cigarette, but never lost that spot. It was his for this night. It would be his until some fool stood in the way, or the lights went out, or until it disappeared as he disappeared. He drank slowly, carefully, savoring the moment, staring. He was almost unaware of her words. He had to ask her to say them again.

"You've been there before," she said. It was the bartender. She was cleaning a tray of glasses. "That spot, you've been there before," she said, dipping a glass in water. "You've been to every spot in this bar. Every single one," she said.

He took a long drag from his cigarette, exhaled, letting the smoke fall away from his mouth, keeping it down and away from their eye contact. "Yeah, I guess I have," he said.

"I've been meaning to talk to you. You come in here once or twice a week. You have your drink and you find your spot. Every now and then somebody'll come up and say something to you and you'll answer but you'll never really answer. You're occupied and you don't want to talk. Seems like all you really want to do is get back to that spot. Well, you've been to that spot before. There's no place else in this bar to go. Talk." She pulled the glass from the water, twisted it on the scour brush and told him her full name. She dried her hand and extended it to him. He placed his cigarette on the ashtray in front of him and for the first time in nearly two years, touched more of her than an errant finger. He felt obliged to tell her his name, so the words kept coming. And as she talked and talked, he listened and commented just enough to keep her talking, adding a fresh detail every now and then just to keep her interested enough not to walk down to the other end of the bar. He took a drag from his cigarette, hit the Jack's one more time.

He found a spot for the evening, a brand new spot. Her voice was intoxicating, and as her lips moved they seemed to entice the jukebox to play side one of *Kind Of Blue*, and as the music came alive, all those autographed pictures, every spot two years observed slid behind to accentuate the emoting melody of her voice. He had found a spot for the evening, a spot that could last for a while. And if he was very careful and didn't make himself too ordinary too fast, he might even get lost in there, or at the very least, get a free Jack Daniel's to help him on his way.

Ten Bottles Til Saturday

He was asleep, deeply, then awake, and asking, "Where am I?" He glanced quickly to his right. A door, open. To his left, a window, the blinds drawn, the sun clawing, breaking through. It was Sunday. He knew it was Sunday, Sunday morning. It was worst on Sunday morning. He never knew where he'd wake up on any given Sunday, but he would glance over to his left, to the bedstand beside him. A bottle, half empty, would wait. It did. He took a drink, then another. With another, she emerged, slowly, mellifluously from the night before.

She slipped into the bed beside him, turned away. The sheet defined her. She was. She had always been. He couldn't let her have this time, so he apologized, silence, again, he apologized. Again, silence. He took another drink, then another, and with another, she reached out and kissed him deeply, passionately. She kissed him, kissed him, filled him, filled him so completely that the bottle became unnecessary, so completely, that he thought he could make it without the bottle in his hand, but as always, as he placed the bottle on the bedstand beside them, as the bottle left his hand, and he reached out for more of her, the sheet would fall, empty. It would take another couple drinks to fill the sheets again, another couple drinks to get out of Sunday morning, and all the bottles he could find to get back to Saturday night.

HEADACHE

He came home with a headache that day wondering where the pills were, wondering why the pills were so fucking hard to find when he wanted them, when he needed them, "Goddamnit! Goddamnit!" he repeated. Those pills were almost in his way anytime he didn't need them, but whenever he did, whenever they were an absolute necessity, whenever his eyelids were on fire, igniting then incinerating the butane-soaked jelly that was passing as the thinking mechanism that was suddenly too big for the inside of his head and was trying to escape every time he moved his hands, his feet, his eyes in a manic attempt to find a moment's relief from the motherfucking fire spike ripping through his medulla oblongata, those goddamn pills were gone. Those goddamn pills were giving their gel-capped calm to some mystery intruder with the single-minded savagery cruel enough to know what was happening in the gas-heated oven furiously attempting to burn its way through the skull of the nigger searching. "Save me, goddamnit! Save me!" he said, but there was nothing to be found. The store was two blocks away, and by this time, no pills were gonna help anyway.

Reflections in the Shower Curtain

The mirror didn't lie. It was him. He looked inside. He touched his face, his cracked lips, it was him, meat sucked away, flesh inside, outside. It was him. It wasn't that nigger he was supposed to be laughing at down on Broadway. It wasn't that bitch he was supposed to be fucking down on Broadway. It wasn't who it was supposed to be but there was nobody else. He looked in the mirror. He touched his skin. The mirror didn't lie. It was him.

Hands hard, burned by glass on fire, eyes distant, searching, always searching through red — fighting to stay open now looking at that little white chip he knows is soap but might not be this time. It might not be and there just might be a hit on that, but no. No, goddamit, he looked in the mirror. It wasn't that nigger down on Broadway. It wasn't that fool. It was this fool. The mirror didn't lie. It was him.

It was the same nigger with too many square inch ziplock bags in his pockets. It was him. The mirror didn't lie. It was the same nigger with that cigarette shaped, black-tipped glass pipe in his left hand, always in one hand, always in his hands. The mirror didn't lie. It was him. It was the same nigger who spent the last bit of his old reflection on a minute away. The mirror didn't lie. The mirror didn't lie, so he turned his back to the mirror, dropped to his knees and picked up that little maybe something of soap. He rolled it around in his fingers until he saw a rock in his hands.

The mirror didn't lie, so he stared at the translucent shower curtain now in front of him. He took a hit. He took a hit. He needed lies. The mirror didn't lie.

FORGIVEN BY THE CLOUDS

His lady was staring out the window when he made it home. They lived on the third floor, but when her eyes were open, she could see everything. She could see everything he did. She was staring out the window. She could see everything. She could see that beautiful young girl in his arms, she could see her soft unscarred skin. She could see her mind behind clear brown eyes, her mind not yet clouded by drugs, not yet clouded by his fist. She could see that beautiful young girl in his arms when he made it home. He kissed that girl deeply before going upstairs. He gripped her ass with both hands. He told her to wait, sat her down, and walked away, upstairs, upstairs to the third floor, upstairs to his lady.

His lady was staring out the window when he opened the door. The door was still open when she started screaming, "Fuck you! Motherfucker! Fuck you!" She was trying to hold back tears that were coming too hard, trying to make a fist that was never hard enough, trying to keep a control that he held tightly in his hands.

"What's the matter, baby?" he said.

"Fuck you, motherfucker! I saw that bitch!"

He just got calm, walked to his lady, grabbed her by the wrists, pulled her close and whispered, "You been hittin' that pipe too long. You ain't seen a goddamn thing." But she could see everything when her eyes were open.

"I saw everything. I was looking right at you, motherfucker. Fuck you!"

His voice went dead. His voice got calm. His voice became a cloud hiding a fist, a fist that made her fingers hard, a fist that made her body scared, a fist that made everything a nothing in clouds. He slammed the door. "You ain't seen shit." And in his voice, the clouds arrived. She yanked away from him, stepped back, and tried to look out the window.

"She's still out there," she said, but there were clouds in the room, her mind was clouded, maybe her eyes were closed. She didn't know.

"She's waiting down there," she said, but there were clouds in the room when he grabbed her face, turned it away from the window and said, "Ain't nothing down there. You been hittin' that pipe too long. Now I don't want to hear no more about this."

She could see everything when her eyes were open. She wanted to keep believing that. She wanted to look out that window and see that girl standing there, but when she tried to take a look, "I'm gonna smack the shit out of you," he said. "I'm gonna kick your motherfucking ass," he said. She stood, a head's turn from clarity, her skin too hard, her body scared, her mind clouded. He pulled her close, lifted her skirt, fucked her till they were alone again, until the window was an illusion, and there was nothing three flights down. He got up, threw a cloud on the floor, opened the door and left his lady. She got up and walked to the window when she was sure he was gone.

That girl was waiting for him downstairs. He kissed her deeply, then looked up at his window, at his lady. He kissed that girl again. His lady saw everything from the window. When her eyes were open, she could see everything, but she closed her eyes. She looked away and ran to the spot where he'd thrown his foil-wrapped cloud. She found her pipe and took a hit, took a hit, took a hit, and everything got cloudy where her man was. When she took hits, there was nothing. She was downstairs, soft, unscared, unclouded. There was nothing. She sat at the window looking through clouds, looking through clouds, looking through clouds and waiting for her man to make it home.

Vampire

I thought she was breathing, but it was the air pushed aside by her fall, it was her lungs in permanent exhale, spitting life away, pushing life beyond her reach and creating that five foot four inch, one hundred twenty pound junk sick stain on the sidewalk. It was her blood begging for air, for air, for pennies, for quarters, for spare change, "Spare change please." It was lies, it was love. It was that desperate need for my pimple-scabbed and track-lined arm to reach out and hold her, to extend lifeless meat and bleed, and bleed, and offer a needleless smack she could suck away from juiced down veins guiding that tasty blood from my heart to her lips, from my heart to her veins, from my heart to her heart.

I thought she was breathing, but it was just another one of her lies, another one of the lies she devised to suck the dick of her true love, another one of the lies she devised to escape, to fall, to fall, to fall and rise, smacked up, smacked in, injected. It was another one of the lies she used to stick that needle in, to prick that needle through unclean skin searching for the blue line that's trying to say, "No," that's trying to say, "That's enough," that's trying to say something, but knows what the body needs and infects itself hoping that this time will be the last time, hoping this time will be the end, hoping this time all breath would be sucked into that three-inch syringe never to inhale again.

I thought she was breathing, and I let her fall, I thought she was gonna get up, or I thought she was sleeping, or I thought she wanted my blood, or I thought she was lying. I thought she was lying. I thought she was breathing, but I knew better. I never saw her breathe before. I never saw her breath.

A REFLECTION

He thought the rain was falling hardest where he was. The abused and broken buildings were surely sucking the water from the sky. Puddles grew beneath his feet waiting for the rainfall, with rainfall they would jump away from the ground, away from the alley, each drop an escape. The puddles beneath his feet would jump, get high, but as quickly as they'd rise they'd fall back into the alley to wait for their next jump. He wondered if there was pain in their waiting. He wondered in pain, waiting.

The rain fell, harder now and more intensely. Things that before were clearly visible, vanished with the fall. The brilliant light of the used car lot at the end of the alley became a blur, a shadow through the translucent wall of water that fell to the alley from the sky. Because of the rain, the alley darkened, and parts once lit by the lot fell victim to the rain, to its shadow. The Italian restaurant three buildings back became a victim. He stood in the five step pit that led to the back door of that restaurant. The pit was flooded to the first step, but he stood, partially sheltered from the rain by the break of the door. A black trenchcoat covered most of his body, and although it was soaked, he was dry all the way down to his ankles. He trembled, not from the cold of the rainfall but from the pain of his dryness, his waiting.

His head dropped. His eyes closed, and for a very small part of a second, he slept. For the remaining part of that second, he was slapped to awakeness. Pain ripped through his inside. He jerked as if he could avoid it, but he couldn't. He tightened his muscles and waited for it to dull. It bent him over, but soon he could stand straight again. He concentrated on standing straight, and the pain became acceptable. As soon as he could think again, he stood on his tiptoes, looked down, the other way. No one was there. No one was coming. No one was coming, goddamit.

The rain slowed. Puddles grew, but there was only waiting. They couldn't escape the ground. The rain fell from the clouds but lacked the power to give freedom from the alley. He looked down at the pit. His eyes adjusted to the dark but he could see nothing beneath him. He could only feel the water as it drained into the five-holed circle at the center of the broken black cement floor. When he could no longer feel the water he stepped into the center of the pit and looked down the alley. The used car lot had a revolving sign. "Lucky Jim's" was on one side. On the other was the time.

He spoke in a whisper, "8:31," still afraid to break his concentration, "where is he?" For a second, he was terrified that the rain had delayed or stopped his smack. He could not allow that thought to last, so he laughed and told himself, "He'll be here in a minute. The motherfucker's just late."

He stood on his tiptoes, looked again, no one. He stepped back onto the break of the door, looked up at the stairs in front of him. When he was certain that he could be seen, he tried to calm himself down. He rocked his body, flexed his arms, scratched his veins. "It's gonna be cool. It's gonna be cool," he said, "he's coming. It's gonna be cool."

He shook the rain off his soaked black trenchcoat and stood, waiting... lightning! He glanced up and it was gone. When he looked down, the pain caught his vacant mind. It ripped through him slowly, much drier than he'd ever imagined possible. He gritted his teeth tightly, until it seemed his upper and lower jaws were one thing. He closed his eyes hard and squeezed a tear from the corner. The pain dulled, but now he was afraid of it. He had to think of something quickly. He had to occupy his mind, so he remembered that the first drop of rain had fallen on him that day. He remembered that the fall had ended on his hand, that the waiting was over for the first drop of rain. There would be no escape. He remembered glancing at the clock at the end of the alley when that drop hit his hand, 7:50. He remembered walking down into the five-step pit of the Italian restaurant, "Shit, it's gonna rain."

But it was raining now. It was 8:33. He was waiting. He didn't want to remember anymore. He got nervous, terrified, and in a voice that was only half a whisper, he cried, "Where the fuck is he?" He stomped up the steps, looked, no one, then the pain. He eased back into the pit, wrapped his arms around his stomach and cried, "Where the fuck is he? Where the fuck is he?"

He reached into his pocket, pulled out a neatly folded roll of bills. It was wet, but the smack wouldn't care. The rain hadn't done any serious damage. Six twenties, a ten, a five, and two ones, all the money was still there. He jammed the roll deeply into the pocket of his black trenchcoat, gripping the bills tightly in his hand. The money had to be there. He'd worked too hard that day. When he thought of his work, he felt a slickness on the bills in his hand. When he realized it wasn't water, he tried to think of nothing, but then there was pain, then a thought erupted, a memory erupted. He was at the northwestern station, hidden in the shadows, behind the broken soda machine where he'd spent most of the day. His black trenchcoat made him almost invisible, and as the people passed, he observed freely, waiting for a moment. Empty, cold, he did not feel. There was only pain to feel, to remind him. His veins were empty. Nothing else mattered. He looked down at the puddle of fallen rain near his feet. He could see himself standing, black, terrifying, a reflection.

The streetlights were dim. They made light circles on the sidewalk but not on the parking lot near the broken soda machine. He stood in shadows, invisible, only he could see. People passed, but only he could see. Every detail was clear to him at first, but as time passed, and his pain grew, things blurred. He fought to see clearly, but it was difficult. People became shapes as the pain grew drier. He fought to see at first, but as the pain ripped free, the end of the pain was all he wanted. People became things that stood in the way of the end of his waiting. He stood, black, terrifying, a reflection pleased that the clouds had formed above, pleased that the night had grown blacker, pleased that the wait would soon be over.

Something in a pink dress passed, but no, two other things followed. A thing in a Bulls cap and its child passed, but no, a car pulled in behind. He stood, dry, trembling, invisible in the corner behind the soda machine, waiting. He saw a three-piece suit walk out of the station. He glanced around. Nothing followed it. The moment had come. In the pocket of his trenchcoat was a .38. He drew the pistol and silently approached that thing from behind.

"Give it up, motherfucker," he whispered, pressing the gun against the back of that thing's neck. When he knew it was intimidated, he took three steps back and said, "Don't turn around. Drop your money on the ground and get the fuck away from here." It said something and that almost made it alive, so "Shut the fuck up," he said, "just give me the goddamn money and get the fuck out of here."

It turned, angry, denied invisibility. A shot was fired and he wanted to stop this memory. He wanted to think of nothing, but there was the pain, then thunder, and he could hear the shot firing. The bullet ripped in, then out, and he could see that three-piece suit fall. He could see it fall face first into the water waiting on the sidewalk, face first into the puddle waiting on the sidewalk. He saw its reflection as it fell, he saw its reflection, and it was a man until he saw the water, until he only remembered the water, the water rising as the three-piece suit landed, the water falling. His veins were empty, his body dry, and there was only water falling to the ground. It had fallen on the money. He reached down, pushed it away, took the wallet, the money, and left the water, the three-piece suit in a memory.

The street was clear. No one followed, so he walked to the bridge. As he crossed it, he removed one hundred and thirty-seven dollars from the wallet. The bills were bleeding, but he couldn't care. His veins were empty and there was pain and the pain was about to stop. He stopped, stared out at the river, when he was sure he was invisible again, he tossed the empty wallet and the pistol into the night black water. It was almost over.

The nearest telephone was on the other side of the bridge. When he saw it, he ran searching his pockets for change. He had just enough for a phone call. The booth was lighted and stood apart from the black of the night. As he approached it the light filled him with anticipation. He pulled the door open and stepped into the light. He knew the number by heart. He put the change in the slot and dialed. A phone rang at the other end. When it stopped and he heard a voice, he started talking. "I got a hundred thirty-seven dollars, man, I need some now, I need some now. You gotta meet me, man. You gotta meet me...."

8:55, the rain poured down again, harder than it had fallen all day. The car lot closed, and after a time, the lights dimmed to black. Soon, nothing in the alley was visible. He stood on the black, waiting. He could do nothing but wait. The pain was there, stronger. The five-step pit that led to the back door of the Italian restaurant three building back of the alley had flooded to the first step again, but he had to sit down. He wrapped his arms around his stomach, stared at his empty veins while sitting in a puddle, in a pit, flooded. The rain fell in a continuously intense stream. He stared at the puddles falling and rising, rising and falling. He wondered if they knew his pain. He wanted them to know his pain.

FUCKING WITH NEEDLES

I kissed her arm, licked bruised vein to the needlepoint, placed my lips on the hole and kissed and kissed until she responded, until the blue of her skin spilled red liquid onto my tongue, until I could taste the remains of her injection and love again.

I kissed her lips, spat the red from my tongue and kissed and kissed until color was replenished, until my breath expanded her lungs, until blue lips and white eyes had the appearance of life and it was okay to make them say, I love you.

I kissed her syringe, placed lips to needle and kissed and kissed until I'd retrieved each drop of blood she'd given, until I could taste her infected soul in my mouth, until all I had to do was open my mouth to release her, or kiss again to love her forever.

Blue Love

Smack is blue kissing untamed love directly to your heart through needles and pins touching blood filled lines painting black skin with red, with red creating color and flesh tones and the means to bend bewitched fingers to inject the light that makes it bright enough to look into her eyes and love her, and love her, and love her unbridled and wild, unbridled and desperate, unbridled and blue.

Smack is blue making sure the tears return, making sure the tears return from longing for her touch, from longing for the memory of her lips caressing your naked heart, the memory of her legs opening to give birth to dreams granted pulse by injected color flowing, injected color falling, color needing, color dying.

Smack is blue, and I'm in love with her diseased touch. I want her inside me. I need her inside me to waste away the time alone in this nightmare, to open my eyes and dream through blood crying for her sweetened breast. I need her inside me to collapse myself into veins searching for her three-inch syringed sword, her syringed sword filled with the love I need to survive. I see her. I see her. I'm flowing to her.

Smack is blue. The needle dies in mid shot touching all the parts only love could touch, painting all of me the color of smack and freezing the moment for the length of love. My arm loses color to the color of blue, but I can see her eyes. I can see her eyes. Smack is blue. Its love is eternal.

BREAKING MY WINGS

I took my needle out, unleashed the smack, but the rush hit me funny. I didn't feel it. I put my tongue to the needlepoint to make sure I didn't get ripped off, but I knew that taste, and it was my death alright. I just didn't feel it this time. I just didn't care this time. I looked at my arms, at the blackened lines, the pimple scabs, the dead veins pumping something that wasn't blood anymore, and I felt a need to see more. I took my shirt off to look at myself. I was almost gone, my chest sunken to a thickened flesh, muscles' impression holding strength in hands only strong enough to push the shooter, to pull the trigger, and bring that death to me, to kiss the side of me and bring that to death. I took a breath to ease the shakes, and then I dropped my pants, pulled them away from me to reveal my leather skinned feet, my legs, my knees scarred or scarred and bleeding from an addiction to living on my knees. I grabbed my dick, and it hid from me, shriveled up past the point of desire, shriveled up, terrified of the thought of reproduction, of creating another me to bleed hungry on the streets of Chicago. I stood naked in an alley behind Halsted and one hundred and something street, and I could feel the smack in my eyes exiting as tears falling down my used and dying body, anointing my deadened flesh, cleansing me with the sight of me and giving a reason to move my foot forward. I moved my foot forward. I didn't stop moving until I was healed.

WHAT I'VE FORGOTTEN

I don't know how to be happy anymore. That's what I was thinking. That's what I was almost saying as I walked down Mission Street past that nigger blocking my way, that nigger with his whole body stain and a smile that entered me, reminded me of needing to smile, then forgetting to smile.

How do you do that? I was thinking. How do you do that? I was almost saying as I walked past that nigger with his needle painted pictures, his pimple scabs, his tracked veins and a leather face twisting, ripping happiness from the broken paradise from a twenty dollar fix injected into lips that still knew how to curl.

I know that smile, I was thinking. I know that smile, I was almost saying as he touched my leg, grabbed my leg, pulled my leg to bring me down, to bring me back down to where he was, to where I'd been, to where I'd been when I could smile, when I knew how to be happy.

"Teach me, motherfucker," I was thinking as I dropped to my knees to taste his lips again. Teach me, motherfucker, I was almost saying as his hands gripped me tighter and I could almost feel his smile in my veins.

"I want to. I want to," I said, but the tears in his eyes reminded me, and I pulled my leg away. I never smiled again.

THE BIRTH OF FLIGHT

The Transfer North

I was on the bus heading south, trying to forget the day, trying to pass anonymously through the night. I was sitting in the back, way in the back, looking, staring at the faces in front of me, at the faces silent, riding. I had a bottle of schnapps hidden in my right pocket. I was taking a hit every now and then, and every now and then, I took a look at the faces, the blank faces, expressionless faces, just trying to get home faces, and I wondered if my face was the same. I took another hit and hoped my face was the same. I looked at the bottle. There was about three-quarters left. When it was empty, I figured I'd be looking like everybody else on the bus. When it was empty, I figured I'd be able to see nothing, feel nothing, think nothing. When it was empty, I figured I'd be able to ignore their faces and ride. When it was empty, I'd be going north just like the rest of the bus. When it was empty, I'd be on the bus, just going north.

The Search for Intelligent Life on the Ave

He walks by with a 9mm automatic pistol dangling slowly in his right hand with a look of intent in his eyes. My hands are empty as I walk past thinking about the two dollars in my pocket and what the fuck I'm gonna do to get myself through the rest of the week. Fear never crosses my mind. Injury never crosses my mind. Death never crosses my mind and it occurs to me that I should not be this insane in this neighborhood, as I walk insane from insanity wondering how I'm gonna get my insanity through the rest of the week.

There's a 9mm automatic pistol dangling in his right hand. If he bends his elbow and curls one finger, I won't have to worry about the sale on potatoes at Lucky's. I won't have to worry about the price of bread rising six cents today. I won't have to worry about what I put inside that bread, but he pays no attention to the lunatic as he heads down the street a little further. Evidently, the dead do not interest him at the moment.

A LAST CHANCE

A shot. Four shots. More, maybe. I thought he was blinking, but his eye vanished, and his skull opened, and he fell to his knees, and he fell face first to the ground and the blood was thick and brown and coming so quickly from his head. The blood was thick and brown and I saw a piece of him shaped like an ashtray fly off and land a couple feet behind him. It was his head open and the piece of skull flying and I thought he was gonna be dead. I thought he was gonna be dead, and I knelt beside him and I called his name. I lifted him by his armpits, and I called his name. I screamed his name as loudly as I could through the tears in my eyes and mouth, and he didn't answer. He didn't answer.

And I thought he was gonna be dead. I thought he was gonna be dead, until I remembered where that piece of skull had landed. I remembered where that piece of skull had landed, and I laid him down gently, and reached over to it. I thought if I could put that piece of skull back on his head, put that piece of skull back on that spot, the blood was gonna stop, the blood was gonna stop and those bullets wouldn't have meant a goddamn thing, the blood was gonna stop, and he was gonna answer me, the blood was gonna stop, and everything was gonna be alright again.

I scrambled over and found that piece of skull and picked it up. It was bleeding in my hands, but I was careful. I cupped my hands tightly to hold the coming liquid. I cupped my hands tightly to keep all of him. I didn't want any of him to slip through my fingers. I didn't want to lose any of him, but when I looked back at his body, twisted and still, there was so much blood, so much blood.

I fell to my knees and through the tears, I could see much blood. I closed my eyes. I opened my eyes, and there were police with guns drawn. In a blink they were everywhere, screaming, shouting. I couldn't understand. I didn't understand. They didn't understand. I had to close the hole in his head to stop the blood, to stop the shots, to hear his voice again, I had to put his skull together. I had to put his skull together or he was gonna be dead. He was gonna be dead. I reached over to him with the pieces in my hand, but they grabbed me. They pulled my arms down and everything fell. Everything fell. Everything fell, and he was gonna be dead. He was gonna be dead, goddamit.

They had to understand. They tried to hold me down but I fought free for a second. I could almost reach him, stop the shots, stop the shots, save him, but they were everywhere. They held me back. I could see him. I could see him. They had their knees on the back of my neck. They cuffed me tight and screamed and screamed. They didn't understand. They didn't understand. I didn't understand. The blood was coming. The blood was coming. I saw that piece of skull. I saw him bleed until he stopped bleeding. Until he stopped bleeding and I understood. A shot. Four shots. More, maybe had been fired, and there was nothing I could do.

A Century East of LAX

He's shooting bullets to the sky, shooting at the planes that pass over him, down Century Blvd. to the airport.

"They're laughing at me," he says. "I can hear them laughing." And the planes pass, chased out of the clouds by bullets fired on Long Beach Blvd. by a nigger child with nothing but bullets to fire, with nothing but bullets to make those planes come down, to make them fight. They pass as his bullets vanish into the sky.

He thinks the laughing is gonna stop. The bullets ring louder than the planes that pass, louder than the laughter he hears, and he thinks the laughing is gonna stop, but the planes vanish into the sky, and there is laughter. He's shooting bullets to the sky, and there is laughter, falling.

The Path of Future Drug Dealers

The children dance defiantly in water stolen innocently to quench a thirst ignited by the too hot summer sun. The hydrant explodes little moments of tyranny, little moments of tyranny falling like rain, little moments of rain falling from a hydrant exploding mercy, soothing mercy, cooling mercy, cooling moments, cooling moments, ecstasy. They dance innocently until blue flashing lights arrive, until blue flexing fist arrives, until blue arrives to give the too hot summer sun the right to burn, until blue arrives to end the tyranny, and the ecstasy, end the crime and return the ecstasy to places unseen, unknown, unreachable. Blue plugs the hydrant, and the children burn in the too hot summer sun. The children burn. The children burn. The children burn until one decides to cool himself. Until one decides to dance again, until one decides to explode the hydrant and bring ecstasy. One decides to explode the hydrant and end innocence.

Burn, Baby, Burn, Said My Baby

My baby wants to shop, but the Fedco's burning. La Cienega Blvd.'s on fire cause some nigger got his ass beat so bad that black itself was screaming, so bad that black inhaled the city and breathed fire, so bad that the sale on underalls had to be delayed for the moment, but my baby had a coupon.

My baby wants to shop. My baby's got to shop, but goddamn those niggers, they breathed in the Fedco. The Fedco's burning. The air's on fire outside the door, but I look at my baby's hand. She's holding that coupon tight.

My baby wants to shop. The Fedco's just a light in the sky, but she don't give a fuck. Some white boy's getting his motherfucking ass kicked on Florence to the chorus of innocently observing news helicopters. She don't give a fuck. There's a tank rolling down Hoover Street. She don't give a fuck. The AM/PM on four corners just exploded scattering slurpees and two-for-a-dollar hot dogs all over any street higher than Martin Luther King Blvd. She don't give a fuck. My baby's got a coupon. There's a sale on underalls. My baby wants to shop. Fuck the flames. Fuck the world. Fuck justice. My baby wants to shop, my baby's gonna shop.

Kids Today

Mr. Johnson had a store out on the corner, probably there when all of us were born. He used to sit outside and watch us come alive, said he loved to watch the children grow.

Mr. Johnson had a store out on the corner. I tried to steal some candy from his bin. He called my mama up. My mama whipped my butt, made sure I never stole from him again.

Mr. Johnson had a store out on the corner. Used to keep an eye on all the kids. Old Johnson called 'em thugs, saw 'em selling drugs. Said we don't need no shit like that 'round here.

Mr. Johnson had a store out on the corner. Robbed a lot of times in all the years, shot six or seven times. So he bought a .45, killed a kid but didn't shed a tear.

Mr. Johnson had a store out on the corner. Wife got shot a couple of weeks ago. Johnson blamed us all. No mamas left to call. Calling mamas just don't work no more.

Mr. Johnson had a store out on the corner. Least until a couple of days ago. There's boards on all the walls where he wrote "Fuck you all. I don't believe I love you anymore."

Prayers for Salvation While Riding to the Promised Land

I'm screaming in your ear on the 22 bus. I'm falling south, but we're moving north from the Mission through to the Fillmore. I'm telling you about the gun in my hands, about the gun I could place to the back of your head, about the gun I could use to retaliate, but my hands are trembling. I'm telling you about my trembling hands on the 22 bus heading south through the Mission to the Fillmore. I'm screaming in your ear, but I wonder if you're listening. I'm telling you about how I tried to make my stand, about how I tried to get my dick hard, about how I tried to survive with this .38 strapped and loaded, aimed to fire, but my hands are shaking, and now they're bleeding, spilling blood on the seat behind you on the 22 bus.

I'm heading south through the Fillmore. I'm screaming in your ear, but it sounds like a whisper. It sounds like another fool, another nigger talking too loud, making his presence known for the length of a ride, another nigger making his existence a reality, an echoing memory in your ear, in the ears of all who can't help but listen. Listen to me. Listen to me, I've spared your life, so I'm screaming in your ear on the 22 bus heading south through the Fillmore to McAllister, to McAllister, just McAllister. I'm screaming in your ear. I'm bleeding from my chest. Your hands are wet with my blood, but I'm alive for this moment, alive but born dead on the seat behind you, born dead as the bus moves down Hayes...Grove...Fulton...listen to me. Listen to me. I didn't shoot back. I'm running out of time.

The Birth and Death of Flight

I read about Bruce in the paper. Three niggers from his building held him down and cracked his skull with a tire iron. He had a two foot screwdriver in his back pocket, so I figured he was trying to get those wings back. Seems like that's all he did since that night passed. I gave up looking for those wings a couple of years ago, but it took six months in jail, two bullet holes, and four ass kickings, including the one that killed him, for Bruce to forget. It took everything to forget that flight could be achieved, that hell was a place below the expressway reserved for the dead, for those who could not fly, for those who could not find the wings, but he could fly. He knew how to fly away from 125th and Halsted Avenue. He'd done it before. He'd done it once before, and he couldn't forget. He wouldn't forget.

He woke up at 3 a.m. that night banging on my window talking about how he just got out a car with some niggers from his building, bout how they showed him what to do when you want a car and you ain't got the keys, the pink slip, or any legal right to have it. I thought this could be valuable information, so I got dressed and walked with him about 10 or 15 blocks to about 110th Street and Parnell where we saw this golden black BMW. It was perfect but the doors were locked, so I looked around for a loose brick and smashed the window.

We hop in. Bruce pulls out a screwdriver and starts prying shit out of where the ignition key goes. After a couple seconds, he starts the car and we're gone. Bruce is driving. We're moving down Halsted. I roll the window down to eyeball all those niggers on the street, and we're just as big as they are, but we ain't bigger until I look to my right. I see a flash, and I think it's the cops, so I start screaming, "Cops! Cops!" Bruce pushed the gas down as far as it went, and from that moment on, we ceased to be human. As the car accelerated, it was as if we had been lifted to another world. There was no one, nothing on the street. There was only forward and it swerved to the left. As we swerved to the left, we entered the expressway. It was as empty as the Halsted Avenue we had elevated from. I glanced out my window, and we were above the streets we lived on our entire life. Every home, every building was obvious. We knew every boarded window, every painted stain, every piss puddle, and as we accelerated down the expressway everything smelled of permanence, of failure. Every home, every building seemed lighted with faces, hungry, desperate, and angry, angry and extending jointed fingers to touch us, to grab us, to call us back and close the walls we'd opened with our sudden acceleration. I could feel them reaching me, trying to pull me back so I screamed, "Faster, motherfucker, faster."

And he stepped on the gas, and we were airborne, flying down an empty expressway to a point beyond any touch we'd known, to a point where the hands calling us were unfamiliar, higher, just out of reach. I could almost see them. I could almost touch them but grabbed the wheel. I turned the wheel and the car landed, spinning, flipping, turning, it landed.

When we'd stopped falling, we looked up, our flight of revelation was burning for its sin, and we had been tossed, relatively uninjured to the streets below. We watched that BMW burn from as far north on Halsted Avenue as we'd ever been. We caught the bus back home, and today, three years later, Bruce is dead and I haven't been that far north since that night. I'm staring out the window, looking at the expressway. I hear a banging, then a broken window. There's a nigger pissing in the alley. Marking his territory, I guess.

"At least his world is smaller than mine," I say. Then I smile.

FOOL

When the dream started, I could hear him laughing at me bending his knee to accelerate, slapping his foot to the floor with a jerk, laughing, laughing like all the applause signs on all the sitcoms in all the world had been flipped on and glued into a constantly blinking command demanding a response to my pants being pulled down to reveal the permanent wet shit stain had to be acknowledged by everyone in the vicinity of 85th and Hoover Street, everyone but me.

"Shut up, motherfucker. Shut up motherfucker," I was saying but the dream was just starting, we were picking up speed, turning left and away from 88th Street, and my voice was silent now, choking on smoke rising to fill the front seat, rising from the area surrounding my right hand muted by the ringing in our ears, but I could hear him laughing, laughing so loudly, so contentedly, I felt the sudden need to shut that motherfucker up, to place my hands around his motherfucking throat and shut that nigger up, shut that nigger up just until this dream was over, just until I'd never met this nigger before and there was nobody laughing on the seat beside me as we slid down L.A. streets escaping, escaping the dream beginning, ending with shots fired when I closed my eyes and heard him laughing, laughing. I reached for his throat, but my hand was heavy.

My hand was full, too full to place around his throat, too full to stop him from saying, "You did it, motherfucker. It's all over now." I opened my eyes and saw the pistol in my hands. "It's all over now," he said, laughing, laughing, laughing, as we slid away from what I'd done. "What the fuck are you laughing at?" I said, but with every conscious blink, with every accidental nap, with every evening R.E.M., I would be a killer again. The dream had started, and he was laughing at a fool.

PARTY

This is how it happened. He wanted to fuck that big-tittied bitch from Crenshaw, but she was trying to come across as some kind of nice girl who wasn't gonna give that ass when she sees a nigger with a roll of twenties, so he calls his cousin up and sets up this party, thinking she might let him slip in there with a little Ole English and some quiet storm, but his cousin calls up a lot more people than that nigger thought and the next thing you know, the word's on the street and that motherfucking house is ten deep in niggers.

Me and the boys was hanging out at that liquor store on Fifty-Third and Broadway when we heard the music. I looked down the street and saw that big-tittied bitch from Crenshaw going in there with a couple of her friends. She had this tight miniskirt on and I said, "Fuck, man, it's time to party!" So I slammed down about forty ounces of mad dog in about forty seconds and went on over there. I still had a couple sips left, so I still had the bottle in my hand when we got to the door. That nigger's cousin was charging two dollars, but fuck that shit. I just walked right in.

The music was pumping and me and the boys was about ready to get nasty when I see that nigger and that big-tittied bitch from Crenshaw moving into the kitchen. Everybody's dancing so it takes me a while to get through the crowd, but when I do, I see that nigger with his hand in that bitch's panties, so I knock out the last couple sips from that forty ounce and smash that bottle on the back of that nigger's head. There's beer and blood and shit all over the floor, and that bitch starts screaming, so I tell her to shut the fuck up and I'm about ready to kick her motherfucking ass when that nigger's cousin comes in with a .38 in his motherfucking hand. He's talking some shit, so I pull out my 9mm and I got three bullets in his head before he finishes a sentence. I walk out of the kitchen with a 9mm in my motherfucking hand, and that's when things got weird.

Everybody was still dancing. Half the niggers were gripping some bitch's ass while slow grinding to Luther, some were sippin twenty ounce cans of Ole E while trying to slip their hands down some bitch's pants, some were just chillin' in the corners. That big-tittied bitch from Crenshaw was still screaming in the kitchen. Somebody went over there and closed the door. And everybody kept dancing. I had to push my ass through that motherfucking floor cause they were still dancing. Nothing changed. Everybody still wanted to fuck. It was a party. Shit happens. Shit happened. That's how it happened. That's how it happens at parties. Some niggers will do anything for pussy.

SHOOTING, KILLING, DRUG BUSTS, COVER-UPS, FUCK-UPS, LIGHTER SIDES, WEATHER, AND SPORTS

"Wake me up at eleven," she says. "I want to watch the news," she says. I let her sleep all night. She asks me why.

"You know," I say, "you need a better reason to wake up," I say.

ANOTHER IMPOSTOR

"I'm an African," that's what he said. He was standing on the corner of 95th and Broadway screaming, "I'm an African," to anybody who could hear, the cars passing by could hear, the lady with the cats and the plants could hear. The kid with the rock wrapped in foil under his tongue, he could hear. The cops rolling up and down Broadway, they could hear.

"I'm an African. I'm an African," he was screaming. And the john in the alley busted a nut. The john he was with asked for a napkin. And the Johnson kids turned up the volume, so they could hear every word the TV said. And the old man across the street took a hit from his bottle of Cisco making sure he kept it in the bag.

"I'm an African. I'm an African," screamed that nigger. And he'd listen, then scream again. And no one questioned him. No one sniffed him for the odor of fresh elephant. No one asked him who Mandela was. No one pointed him in the direction of home. And if they didn't have to, no one even bothered to look at that nigger.

"I'm an African," was the scream. And no one opened their doors. And no one missed a step. And no one made it a point to hear that noise. He was on 95th and Broadway now. 95th and Broadway. He looked like he was home.

Leaving the Comforts of Home

I moved north, past that couch in front of the Shell station on the corner of Century and Broadway, past that fucked-up mattress with the cotton hanging out and all over that alley between Figeroa and Hoover, past that blood stain on that colder street sidewalk, that blood stain that somebody was supposed to clean up, but everybody just ignored.

I moved north. Past that Manchester Blvd. whore with the cum-stained miniskirt and the birth cleansing aroma of urine. I moved past that nigger on 76th Street, that nigger behind the laundromat, behind the dumpster, behind the bic lighter flame, the glass pipe and cloud of smoke that seemed to suck his flesh away. I moved past that boy he knows, that boy on the bicycle, that boy with his mouth full and change for a thousand, that boy riding to that back house about a hundred feet away from the 110 freeway.

I moved north, past my sister crying welfare on Florence Ave, past my brother crying culture on Slauson Ave, past my mama crying God on Vernon Ave. I moved north, where Tam's Burgers were, McDonald's were, swap meets were, shopping malls and liquor stores were, B of A's.

I moved north, where niggers were mostly on TV, getting their ass kicked and deserving every skull smashing blow, where niggers were so fucking stupid you could see why nobody trusted them, where you know what that nigger was in this neighborhood to do.

I moved north. The U-Haul was empty. I left my world behind to buy everything north of home.

He Called Me Spiderman

I got home about 3 a.m. that night. I was only half drunk. I wanted to be all drunk, but the bars and liquor stores closed before I could finish the job, so I had to settle for just feeling good, and I was feeling good. I even said "Hi" to the kid on my front stoop playing with his Spiderman doll as I went into my pocket looking for my keys. I found my keys and glanced over again. There was another doll, a Doctor Octopus doll. The kid was holding his Spiderman doll and kicking the shit out of that other doll.

"Kick his ass, Spiderman," I said as I opened my door and stepped inside. I was about to lock up when I finally realized what the fuck I just said. I glanced out the door again and looked up at the sky. The moon was there. It was a 3 a.m. moon. The street was still, mostly quiet, just like a 3 a.m. street, and I was tired, almost as drunk as I like to be at 3 a.m., but when I looked down at my front stoop, something mid-afternoon was happening. The six-year-old boy from the apartment next door was playing superhero outside, and it had to be way past his bedtime. I stepped outside.

"Where's your mama, boy?" He shrugged his shoulders and kept beating the hell out of that Doc Oc doll.

"Ain't you supposed to be in bed?" I said. He shook his head 'no' then, with the aid of Spiderman, smacked old Doc into the street and with his best superhero voice said, "Yeah, motherfucker. You fucking with Spiderman, now."

Then he gets up and charges his hero doll into the street after his supervillain. He pulls it out from under a parked car and smacks Doc Oc again and again and again until that kid's halfway down the block bringing justice at the hands of Spiderman to a silent street at three o'clock in the morning. I ring the bell next door. No one answers. I knock on the door as loudly as possible that late at night. No answer. I try the lock. It's open. I step inside.

"Hey. Hey lady. Your kid's out here in the street." But nobody's home.

I step outside and look down the block. The kid's sitting in the middle of the intersection with his two dolls. I go back into the apartment next door looking through rooms for his mama, but she still ain't home, so I open their kitchen window, stick my head out.

"Hey, boy, get out of the fucking street." He acts like he doesn't hear me and keeps on playing, so I just say, "Fuck you. Get your ass run over then."

And he takes his hero doll and smacks that crook over some parked cars and onto the sidewalk. Then his superhero voice starts, "Now you must die, nigger." And with Spiderman in his hands charging forward for the next mighty confrontation, the kid squeezes through two parked cars and sets off an alarm. He sits beside the screaming vehicle with the two superdolls trading blows. A light comes on two buildings down. And someone inside shouts, "Get away from my car. I'm calling the police."

The kid just sits there playing hard. I don't know when his tears started. I just saw him wiping his eyes between each power blow delivered in the name of heroism, wiping his eyes with Spiderman in one hand protecting him from the evil in the other hand, sniffling, trying to make Spiderman save the world. It might have been that boy's tears or it might have been my half-filled body of alcohol, or it might have been Spiderman's head popping off during one especially vicious blow, but I felt a sudden urge to spring from that window and crawl down and out of our building. I had no time to find my disguise. I had to hold that boy. I had to make him feel like he wasn't alone out there at 3 o'clock in the morning. I had to make him feel safe in spite of my slightly inebriated state.

I slid down the gutter and made one powerful step towards him, but that's when I heard the sirens. That's when the reality of the situation hit me. That's when I realized I was a drunk ass nigger trying to embrace a six-year-old boy at 3 in the morning with no mothers in sight and the police less than four blocks away. That's when I realized I was lacking the wall crawling, web shooting, super strength to save this child. I was too late. I was too drunk and I was going back to our building to find a drink. I looked back once. I looked back to see that six-year-old on the streets with his hero in his hand, and the police approaching. Spiderman's head rolled down the sidewalk to my feet as I walked away. I knelt down and stuffed it in my pocket. I didn't have to look at it to know my secret identity had been revealed. Doc Oc smacked the headless Spiderman into the building next door, and from what I can see from a lengthening safe distance, he's making a big comeback. Two cops surround that kid, and he's alone out there at 3 in the morning. I close the door to my apartment, take Spiderman's head from my pocket and looking it in the eyes, "You ain't gonna save a soul tonight," I say, then go to the refrigerator looking for the Miller's I sometimes leave in the back.

PSALMS WRITTEN DURING THE
VIOLENT DEATH OF BRUCE JACKSON

Riot at Winchell's

I want his doughnut. He was eating that fucking donut the first time he kicked my ass. He's gonna be eating that doughnut again. I want his doughnut. I used to walk by wanting that doughnut. I used to walk by wanting a taste. Now I'm gonna have a taste. I want his doughnut. I want what makes him stay here. I want his jellies. I want his glazed. I want his chocolate caked, and anything, anything that makes him stay. I want his doughnut. I know there's gonna be trouble. I know there's gonna be a fight. I may put fresh bakery items at risk when I get my ass kicked this time, but I want his doughnut. I see his gun. There are little white frosting prints on the trigger. I see his badge. There's a drop of custard staining the metal. I see blue. I see black. I see white. They're a striking contrast to the pink box full of fantasies he's been teasing me with. I want his doughnut. He's waiting for me, powdered sugar stains on his lips and fingertips, my flesh, my bloodstains at the ends of his billy club. I'm gonna get my ass kicked again, but I want his doughnut, and he won't give it to me.

The Final Attack of the Blues

Ain't nowhere to run now, nigger. The billy clubs are out. You're surrounded, halt! or they'll shoot. Mama can't help you now. Ain't nobody to call. They're closing in. Somebody just dialed 911 and it's your ass, motherfucker.

Ain't nowhere to run now, nigger. You're a white cop's fantasy. He don't need a burning cross. He don't need a swastika. He don't even need a white hood today. Blue's gonna due today. It's all he needs to beat your motherfucking ass. It's all he needs to get his dick hard. It's all he needs to be the man.

Ain't nowhere to run now, nigger. Stand or fall. Get your motherfucking ass up, or you're gonna be somebody's bitch, get your motherfucking ass up, or everything you've got is theirs. Get your motherfucking ass up, and at least die standing. Get your motherfucking ass up and be free til they get here.

Ain't nowhere to run now, nigger. They're knocking on the door. A warrant has been issued, but your partners, your lady, your children are watching. Ain't nowhere to run now, nigger. They're kicking the door down. The cuffs are out, but your gun is loaded, your gun is aimed, your dick is hard. You must be a man, your dick is hard, you must be a man! Ain't nowhere to run now, nigger man! They've opened the door, "What do you want, motherfucker?"

Nigger Sleeping on a Bus Stop Bench Somewhere in America

"Wake up," he said. But I was asleep. Night had fallen and it was time to sleep. The world was sleeping. I closed my eyes.

"Wake up, goddamnit." But it was night for me, too. I had the right to close my eyes. I had the right to sleep with the rest of the world, to see nothing with the rest of the world. I closed my eyes to be with the world. I closed my eyes to be with the world.

"Get your motherfucking ass up!" he said, but I clung to the silence of unconsciousness. I refused to hear and imagined myself drifting on that evening, drifting to that compliant fall to daylight, to that eye opening awareness of the sudden stop below.

"Get the fuck up, nigger." But I fought the urge to wake. I fought the urge to stand, to separate myself from the world, to open my eyes. I closed my eyes. Night had fallen. I slept with the world. I slept with the world, and when he beat me, when he killed me, when he tried to separate me, I kept my eyes closed. The world was sleeping, and with my eyes closed, I would sleep with the world. Nothing was gonna stop me. I slept with the world.

DRAGGING BABY SCREAMING INTO DAYLIGHT

We were making love when we heard the gunshots, so we didn't stop, a stray bullet entered our bedroom, shattered our window, opened the plaster above us and puffed white powder on our backs, but I could feel her fingernails digging deep into my spine, so I pulled myself closer, slid an arm beneath her ass and stayed inside. We had work to do. Teenage worlds were ending, unprepared for the injected explosions igniting inside them and barely 50 feet from our embrace, teenage worlds were screaming, "Fuck you" to the angel of death coming to take them away in a blaze of blue spit fire, teenage worlds were ignorantly flashing what would be that last hardened dick, calling out what would be that last touch of living, breathing ecstasy to the muted echo of my love pulling me closer to her, inhaling that call bringing it inside her as the gunfire echoes, echoes, echoes, and stops, and we've retrieved a falling fragment of the drifting life in the air, we lay still, waiting, waiting for the sirens to arrive.

We got out of bed when we saw their lights flashing on the shattered glass on the dresser and floor. I looked out through what once was our window. Three more babies dead or dying. The police observing in force. One looked up and directly into our window, me and my lady were still naked. Her arm was around my waist, and my dick was still hard. That cop saw all of us but locked on my eyes. Another cop approached him talking.

"Looks like a few more dead homeboys," he said.

"Yeah," said the other cop, never leaving my eyes, then smiling, smiling, "but they'll make more," he said. "They'll make more."

The Scream of Our Shadows

They wanted to know who shot that cop, so they took our doors away, put footprints on locked doorknobs, bloodstains in peekholes, and left a trail of boot-splintered wood up and down our avenue. They took our doors to make us naked, naked to all eyes, naked to blue, so blue could see, so blue could look inside and find the trigger pulling hatred that shot a scream into the sky and hit a cop.

They wanted to know who shot that cop, so they took our doors away. They took our inside away, made the outside blue, and we could see their fist-shaped questions yanking us outside to be delivered on the dirt patched yards in front of us. We could see their billy-clubbed questions beating pleas for mercy on the alleys beneath where we put our garbage.

We could see their bullet holed questions fired through the perfectly rectangular, man sized spaces kicked into our walls to flatten our doors, to create a low rent exit for fingers firing retaliatory answers, retaliatory screams.

They wanted to know who shot that cop. They asked everyone. Each home bore scars of their questions, and as the blue rolled furiously down the avenue, searching, searching down the avenue illuminated by the light of doorways, by the light of doorways exposed to question, exposed to blue, as the blue rolled furiously down the avenue in the light of doorways, shadows formed. With hands of extended metal finger, shadows formed.

They wanted to know who shot that cop. They took our doors away to see, but we could see when they took our doors away. We could see. The kitchen light flips down the street, and a shadow extends to the sidewalk as its hands curl to fist. The hallway light flips on upstairs, and a shadow extends to the sidewalk as its fingers curl to fist. The living room lamp flips on across the street, and a shadow extends to the sidewalk as our fingers curl to fist engulfing black falling upon the blue on our avenue. There were no doors on our avenue, no doors to hide the shadows, and for twenty feet in each doorway, there was man-shaped black on the sidewalk, man-shaped black staring, seeing the question delivered by blue.

"Who shot that cop?!" they'd ask tearing the answers from the red-toothed bleeding tongue of a silent witness ignorant of the shadows.

"Who shot that cop?" they'd ask beating the answers to obvious vision in the swelled, cracked eyes of a blind witness unaware of the shadows forming.

"Who shot that cop?" they'd ask injecting answers into the back of the skull with the .38 caliber barrel of the law as the shadows rose in dimension from the sidewalks, preparing to scream, preparing to scream.

They wanted to know who shot that cop. They didn't know. They didn't know. We were guilty, and prepared to be guilty again.

In the Mirror, Guarding My Fists

"Just let them take you," he said, with skin torn smooth brown lines creasing his jet black skin speaking in scars, speaking in pains.

"You can't win this time," he said, as I flexed every muscle in my body and fought like a savage to break their grips.

"Just give up," he said with his shoulders lowered and tired, with his eyes beaten and glazed, with his eyes unamazed.

"Don't fight them," he said, as I managed to move one arm, as I managed to pull one of those motherfuckers off of me, as I managed to stand on my legs in spite of this presence on top of me.

"Just let them take you," he said, as the clubs came out and went around my throat, as the clubs came out to beat the savage, as the clubs came out and took the dignity I'd stolen, took the dignity from my clenched hands.

"Just let them take you," he said, as I fell limp, naked, amazed by their power.

"Don't fight them," he said, as they dragged my black away.

"They'll take your fist away," he said.

White Light

When that beam of light hit me, I was running, coming out of that liquor store on 53rd and Broadway, clutching forty ounces of mad dog in one hand, and one hundred and eighty-six blood stained dollar bills in the other. I was running with my shirt out, covering a pistol, fired, hidden in the small of my back, hidden, but touched by my hand with my fingerprints, with five chambers empty, and one bullet matching the caliper and markings of the five bullets fired into that motherfucker who wasn't going to give me nothing.

I was running when that beam of light hit me, blinded me, attached itself to me. Rotated around by the cloud descending to the sound of rotor blades disguised as machine guns' fire, triggered by the Lord calling ratatattat or thaacka thackathackathacka or something like that, and I was listening to the sky, but I was running. I was running when that beam of light hit me, when those headlights appeared from the black outside that pillar of white light slapping the ground beneath my feet.

I was running when I heard those headlights screeching to a halt, screeching to my left, to my right, to my every conceivable route of escape, screeching where my next step was gonna be, to where it wouldn't be, couldn't be, and I had to stop and be that nigger in the middle of a white light, black and obvious, caught in the center of a beam descending. The ratatattat or thackathackathacka got louder as the sky fell down on me. As the beam fell down to slap my black ass into submission, expanding with descent, expanding to give dimension, reality to painted black hoods and opened white doors, red lights flashing, and pistols loaded, readied, aimed...when that beam of light hit me, I was running. "Get on your knees," it said.

"Get on your motherfucking knees," it said. "Get on your knees, goddamn it."

When that beam of light hit me I was running. The sky was screaming.

I looked up and it was coming down on me. "Ratatattat or thackathackathacka, get on your knees," it said. And I clasped my hands together but I would not submit. I grabbed my pistol. God was coming, I figured it was time to pray.

THE BLUE-EYED GODS OF CENTRAL AVENUE

Blue lights flashed and in a moment, I was on my knees.

"FACE DOWN!"

"HANDS ON YOUR HEAD!"

"GET YOUR ASS DOWN, GODDAMNIT!"

"FACE DOWN! DON'T LOOK AT ME! FACE DOWN!"

Compliant, compliant, I pray on my knees to my savior. They kill defiance. I stare forward. He pats me down. He's through my pockets. My keys, my money, my pipe lie beside me, his hands still searching, finding nothing he wants. I stare forward, unable to see, unable to speak, unable to feel. Anger is forbidden. They kill anger. I stare forward. The cuffs are too tight. I lift my hands to show him.

"GET YOUR ASS DOWN, BOY!" My wrists bleed, but resistance is forbidden. They kill resistance. I stare forward. I stare at the walls. Blue lights flash, light the painted names of friends, enemies. So many dead. So much fear. So much to fear. He is strong, angry and strong, breaking me, lighting a fuse, but I stare forward tonight.

The radio: shots fired. Police in need of assistance. And I'm released from the hand of my savior. Free, as the blue lights flash down Central Avenue in search of defiance, in search of anger, in search of resistance. Maybe they'll find it tonight and kill it.

STEPPING ON THE CRACKS

I'm walking their way. I'm dropping my eyes, I'm staying in line, trying not to step on the cracks that break my mama's back. I want to keep my mama safe but they see me in their rearview mirror, they're talking in their radios, unclipping their holsters. They turn the corner. They're coming again. They're coming again, and I'm walking their way, my movements slight, no need to fight, I'm doing right. I'm doing right. I'm staying off the cracks that break my mama's back, but their sirens are flashing, their spotlight's on me, all the curtains on the street open and all those innocent of melanin observe freely as the blue eyed guardians of the unpigmented land above my home make certain that I walk their way, say what they say, conjugate that verb, remember magic words and stay off those cracks that break my mama's back as they tell me to "Dance, nigger." And I must dance their way. I must walk their way, talk their way, keep my eyes down. "Keep your eyes down, nigger." And I keep my eyes down to see. They want to break my mama's back, but I won't step on the cracks. I won't step on the cracks.

The Right Time

If there was something wrong with me, maybe things would have been all right, but there was nothing. I knew that. My mama made sure I knew that. She would stand me up and tell me over and over again, and eventually, I believed her. There was nothing wrong with me. There was nothing to fear from me, nothing to fear that night. There was no wind. The cold was bitter, stationary. It should have moved. Maybe things would have been all right if it moved. Maybe the wind could have caught the snow, and maybe the snow would have blinded things, hid things, faces.

His Mercedes stalled about half a block away from me. It was cold. I was walking, and I wasn't going to stop. He got out of the car and headed for the payphone, the payphone I would have to pass to get to where I was going. There was a light in the booth. There was no wind to catch the snow, so I could see his face clearly. He was a nigger just like me, a nigger about my age, a nigger about my size, my weight, like me, a nigger just like me.

We were the same until he glanced over, until he saw me. If the window would have caught the snow, if the light in the booth would've blown out, if I was born wrong, I would not have remembered the fear in his eyes, the fear in the eyes of that one old white woman in that empty elevator pushing the close door button when she sees me coming. I would not have remembered the fear in that nigger's eyes, the fear in the eyes of the white man behind the desk saying "No" cause he don't know and he don't want to know. I would not have remembered the fear in the eyes of that store owner moving his hand to the .38 under the counter when all I want is a fucking pack of Marlboros.

If something was wrong with me, if the wind would've caught the snow, if the light in the booth would've blown out, if something, anything would've happened to make me miss that look maybe things would have been all right, but the cold was bitter, stationary. There was no wind, so I could see the nigger's face. His face was clear. Things were clear. I was only a step or two away from him. He hung up the phone without dialing, without speaking. He left his change, tried to make it back to his car, away from the nigger behind him, away from me, but there was no escape.

He offered me his money, his wallet, the key to his car, but I wasn't interested in that shit. I wanted him to know what he was doing. I wanted him to know. I hit him hard, and he fell backwards onto the door of his Mercedes. I hit him again and again and again and he didn't fight back. His fear just intensified and froze him. He begged and he pleaded, but that look of fear was still there, so I hit him again.

I hit him again. I hit him again, and then a spotlight hit us from down the block. Blue and red lights flashed, speeding in our direction, but illuminating the terrified eyes of that nigger, that look of fear was still there, so I hit and I hit and I hit. Blue and red lights flashed, and I knew his saviors were coming. I could feel his saviors coming with that same look of fear in their eyes, with that same look of fear in their eyes and their black metal compensators in their unsnapped holsters, with their black metal compensators in their white hands. I could feel his saviors coming, but that look of fear was still in the eyes of that nigger, so I hadn't finished and I hit and I hit and I hit.

He fell, curled, fetal, a baby at my feet. He saw the police coming. He saw the police coming. He saw the police coming, but for reasons he did not yet understand, I was not running but kicking now, kicking now, kicking now. I didn't want to escape. I made no attempt. He wondered why I made no attempt, why I continued kicking and in that moment, the look of fear changed in his eyes, that look of fear changed, and I had something to say to that nigger, but I was clubbed from behind, I fell, and a gun was jammed at the back of my head, my face was slammed to the concrete, and I was chained tight, cuffed tight.

There was blood in my eyes, and I couldn't see his face anymore, I couldn't see his eyes anymore, but I screamed to that nigger, "Now you have a reason. Now you can be afraid." I screamed to that nigger, "Now you have a reason. Now you have a reason." But the wind was blowing now. The wind had arrived. It caught the snow, and I wondered if I could be seen at all, heard at all, through the cold.

A Liquid Mercy

"Police! Open the door." But they were inside. I stuffed my pipe under the pillow with the rock still boiling on the glass. I ran to my bedroom door, but it flung open on me, and blue spilled inside, a cop with pistol drawn spilled inside, liquid spilled inside. He grabbed my wrist, put me against the wall, and cuffed me tight. Two others followed, searching, infecting the veins of my insides, my home. "Is this your apartment?"

"Yes," I said.

"Is there anyone else on the premises?"

"No," I said.

He pointed to a picture on the wall, "Is that your son?"

"Yes," I said.

His eyes moved through me to every part of the room, connected with the blue liquid invading. "Do you have any drugs on the premises?"

"Fuck no! Goddamnit! What the fuck are you doing here? It's three o'clock in the motherfucking morning!"

"Your son's been shot. He's dead." And they were inside. I could feel my blood flow. I could feel blue liquid guiding my bloodflow, searching, I could feel my blood searching for the rock under my pillow.

My son was dead. I needed the rock under my pillow. I could feel my blood moving, searching until blue exited with my rock and my pipe in its hands. He looked into my eyes, my three o'clock in the morning eyes, my just had a pipe hit eyes, my just found out my son's been killed eyes, and he read me my rights. I was unaware of the tears in my eyes until he led me to his black and white, until he led me past my son, through my son, the tears made the blue a wave, a liquid inside my boy, a liquid touching, analyzing, infecting him, a virus changing the color of his blood, slipping into places only the red in his veins should know.

We drove away, and I watched as this liquid flowed through the streets and alleys of my son, filling his bullet holes with blue, rampaging and filling my son, my neighborhood with a liquid to wash it away. And they were inside, and I could feel my blood flow. We were driving away, and I could feel my blood searching. I didn't realize we'd stopped. I didn't realize the door was open until liquid, until blue, until that cop touched me, until he pushed me out and said, "Life goes on."

He drove away, but they were inside. I couldn't stop the flow, so I reached into my son, my neighborhood for a rock and a pipe. And when that rock was boiling, I took a long hit. "Yeah, life goes on," I said, and with blue liquid in my veins, I became aware of the ocean. I dived in. I took a hit.

Straight Time

Just thought back to silence, thought back to the past times when no one knew my name, times when no one asked, times when I could be alone and no one wanted blood, nobody knew if I was dead, nobody cared enough, and I could hear a whisper and recognize a laugh and I could waste my life away and never have to ask.

Just thought back to silence, thought back to my youth, to when my body didn't hurt, before it was abused, to when I didn't think of death, to when I didn't care, before I found out what had passed, before I was aware, and I could hear a whisper and recognize a laugh and I could waste my life away and never have to ask.

Just thought back to silence, to when I'd slip away, to when I'd have to find a vein to make it through the day, to forget about addiction, forget about the weight, forget about the nakedness, the pain of getting straight, to when I heard the whispers, to when I heard the laughs, to when I wasted life away and never had to ask.

Just thought back to silence, but I'm awake again, lock-down is at nine o'clock, the lights go out at ten, niggers screaming all the time, niggers scream in pain, probably thinking silent things in need of better days.

SITTING DOWN PISSIN'

You see, they hold you down. Somehow that cell door opens, and they hold you down. As many as they think it's gonna take come into your cell and hold you down. You don't move. They put you flat. They hold you down. They put you where your dick can't be seen, where you look most like a bitch, face down, ass up, they hold you down. And when you scream, they don't hear a man. They hear that teasing cunt who wouldn't give them no play on the outside. "Shut up, bitch!" "Shut up, bitch!" And they hold you down.

The cell door opens, they hold you down, and you get the same asskicking, the same buttfucking she would have got. The cell door opens and they fuck you until the vision of that bitch becomes real enough to make them cum. And when they're pulling their shit-stained dicks out, denying odor, imagining the smell of her cum, when you have no reason to fight anymore, and they've taken what you've held so tightly for so long, when you can no longer see the cell door open, when you can no longer feel their arms holding you down, do you lie there? "Are you a man or their bitch?" you ask. The cell door's open, "Man or bitch?" you ask. The doors open, opened to hold you down. You see, they hold you down. Do you lie there?

Fucking in the Land of Ice and Razors

I could feel that warm liquid crawling through leg hairs sliding down my inner thigh, a warm razor sliding down to the back of my knee, but it was a cold razor when it touched my calf, when it slid to woolen blanket, soaked through to mattress, to roped springs, when it dropped to concrete, and slid away to an escape beyond the ten bars at arm's length.

"Open your eyes, motherfucker! Open your eyes!" he said. But I knew what I'd see, eighteen-year-old nigger bitch, ten digit prison khaki pulled down to the ankles, asshole pinched, ass pulled up, eyes closed tight, eye closed tight, eyelash fringed, curled lid curtains blinked over blood-lined eyes and seeing everything a blink allows no matter how long closed eyes stay closed.

The lights were out, all cells locked down, and for no fewer than twenty years nothing would change with my eyes open, nothing would change with my eyes open, and those would be his fingers leaving prints on the back of my neck, that would be his fist creating yet another discoloration in my previously untouched nigger flesh. That would be his fist slapping the taste from lips still capable of recognizing the purity of mother's milk. That would be his fist opening my once virgin and untorn asshole.

"Open your eyes, bitch!! Open your goddamn eyes," he said. But I was leaving now. My eyes were closed tight, and I was exiting to the thunder clouds above the bars, the walls, the shotgun blasts. My flesh was alive and screaming, but I was above me, grasping desperately to lightning black razor soft clouds breaking out of the sky. I was in her arms, my hands moving delicately through her flesh and muscle, my lips, my tongue vehemently attempting to slip into her frozen dark, to slip into an escape denied by law for no fewer than twenty years. My arms were around her. My lips were touching her, and I was almost inside.

"Open your eyes, motherfucker! Here I come," he said. He entered, and he entered, and he entered and I could feel that warm razor sliding down my inner thigh, that warm razor slicing down to the back of my knee, opening my flesh and muscle with a liquid ejaculating, sliding down my leg, sliding down my leg until... she was touching me, her soft brown hair smelling of daffodil bulbs, her tender skin a lightning touch from beyond this stone barred prison world. Her lips were blowing cold into my mouth, and the razor sliding down my leg was frozen. It slid, now painlessly, to my calf. She was touching me, and she could never be too far inside.

"Open your eyes," she said. "Open your eyes." I opened my eyes and I was blind. I was blind. Her glacial touch had breathed black into my eyes, and I was blind. I could feel that warm liquid sliding down my inner thigh, but she told me she was cumming again, and I believed her.

THE NIGGER AT THIRTY

I've learned to love the rape, I extend my arms to pull you nearer. I want to kiss your lips. I want to fuck your back. I've got to love you. I love you. I love you. I've learned to love the rape. My ass expands with rips and tears. I lubricate your entry with my blood. My screams of desperation, my screams of humiliation, my screams of hatred have simplified. They are screams of ecstasy, screams of ecstasy. I love you. I love you.

I've learned to love the rape. I'll bend over backwards to lick the caked white cum stains from my ass, I'll squeeze my eyelids together so tightly I'll force warmth into the image of your fuck. I'll kiss the hands that break my neck. I'll kiss the fist that cracks my skull. I love you. I love you.

I've learned to love the rape. I love the rape as your anger builds. I love the rape as you want to kill. I love you, and you kill me but fail.

I love the rape. I win.

TWO WEEKS LATER
FOR ROSIO

This time she saw me slammed up against that black and white taking orders like a good nigger, and the two week stint in County seemed to last a little longer. I glanced back as they tried to tighten those cuffs through my wrists, and that confused, that embarrassed, that disgusted look on her face seemed to stick with me through every minute of the fourteen days I spent in that fifteen hundred room nigger-making cage down at the bottom of deep downtown L.A.

I spent the last three days of my as yet to be determined imprisonment staring at the intercom waiting for my name to be called. It was getting close to 1 a.m. when I finally heard it. I was in that half-sleep you only get at the county jail when you're in on some 'fucking with you' bullshit, and they gave you thirty days to scare your black ass into doing what you're told, but you know all the cells, all the dormitories, all newly converted, fifty portable bunk TV rooms are full, are overflowing, and you know you ain't gonna be under lock and key much longer.

They called my name again and I smiled. I closed my eyes and as I let go of all the concrete air inside me, I could see the sidewalk leading to her apartment. I could see the doorway opening. The light revealing her, the light revealing me, the light went on in the fifty bed TV room and all the niggers whose names hadn't been called tried to hide under their county-issued sheets and covers, all but the ten niggers with my matching smile. They were tapping sleeping eyes trying to sell leftover smokes, trying to collect overdue debts, and receiving messages to be delivered personally to the outside. I, however, was still in my bunk. I still had my eyes closed. I was trying to get up that sidewalk, to open that door all the way and change that look on her face and make her see that I was not the monster L.A. County was making me out to be, that I was not the crack smoking, drive by shooting, bitch beating animal they wanted her to believe I was. I closed my eyes and dreamed a little longer to make her see that I was still just a victim of circumstance. That the look on her face was unnecessary, and it was still okay to touch me. It was still okay to touch me. I felt a kick on the leg of my bunk.

"They ain't gonna call you again, fool." It was the nigger on the bunk next to me, "You better get your ass outta here and give me that pack of smokes you been hoarding." I sat up, put my feet on the floor, then handed him two of my six rolled Bugle Brand cigarettes. I stretched my arms up and back until I heard a nice relaxing pop.

"I guess you gonna find out now, boy," he said.

"What the fuck you talking about, nigger?" I say.

"That bitch you was up there dreaming about. I guess you gonna find out now," he says.

"Find out what?" I say, and he turns away from the light, gets under the sheets and covers all the way, but I can hear him laughing, laughing like he knew something only niggers under permanent lock and key were privileged to know, something he no longer felt a need to share with a nigger about to be free, a nigger like me. A nigger about to walk up that sidewalk, open that door and find out how long two weeks has been.

FLOWERS IN STRYCHNINE

"Tell me how to keep her, Mama. I don't know how to keep her," he said, the sound of the phone shaking in his hand, losing volume in the 5000 miles of distance between ears, in the sound of his children crying on one end of the line and his father sleeping loudly on the other.

"Tell me, Mama," he said. "Tell me, Mama," he said.

"Did you hit her, boy?" she whispered.

"No, Mama, but it's 3 a.m. and she just got home."

"That don't mean nothing, don't you hit her."

"I don't want to hit her, but some nigger just called asking me where she was."

"Don't you hit her."

"But she's packing a bag. She's leaving me. She's taking the kids. How do I keep her? How do I keep her, Mama?"

"Don't you hit her. Beating that woman ain't gonna make her stay," she said still whispering.

"You're wrong, Mama."

"I ain't wrong, You're a man. You hit that girl, you're gonna hurt her, and she's gonna leave you."

"You're wrong, Mama. She wants me to hit her. She's in my face real close, so close I can smell that nigger on her. She's got her finger in my face and she's yelling at me like I'm a three-year-old child whose ass she can whip any time she feels a need to get that nigger's smell again. She don't give a fuck that the kids are in the room, listening, crying. She wants me to hit her. She wants me to hit her. How can I keep her now? How can I keep her, Mama?"

"Let her go, boy," she whispered.

"No, goddammit! We have children, I love her. I need her. Tell me how to make her stay. Tell me how to make her stay, Mama."

"I don't know, boy," she said in a voice meek and whispering tears.

"You do know, Mama, you do know." And he dropped the telephone. His mother was still listening when the first fist landed. She whispered his name again and again, but she only whispered. She didn't want to wake his father. She shed a tear each time she heard a fist and thought back to when he was a child, listening, crying through sixteen years of Daddy making Mama stay. "Like father, like son," she thought. "Like father, like son." She glanced over at the man beside her, his father. He stirred and placed his arm around her waist. He had her. She could never leave. His eyes opened. She would never leave.

THE CHILD GROWS OLD

Take off your glasses, she says. I want to see your eyes, she says. Poor baby. You have the eyes of a child, she says. You have the eyes of a child, and we made love. We made love as she looked into my eyes. You have so much distance, she says. You have so much time, she says. You make me cry, she says. Poor baby. Poor baby. And I closed my eyes. I was so tired, I thought I'd see forever. Beaten so badly, I thought it had to be almost over. I had aged so long, I thought I could rest my eyes, but she stared into my eyes. Poor baby. Poor baby. You have the eyes of a child, she says. You have the eyes of a child.

Burning the Cum Stains in the Closet

The bed was the first thing out the window. It landed upright with the mattress still on the box spring, and the pleated sheet still intact, the other sheets and blankets lying on the sidewalk as if kicked off by the evening's activities. Only a few pieces of wood on the box had been broken. The bed was ready for action in spite of its three story fall, but most of the things they owned couldn't handle that fall. The stereo, the TV, the VCR, all that shit was shattered, scattered along the street below. He had an elaborate picture in his head.

They were fucking right there, in his room, in his bed, fucking to the rhythm of his brand new Neville Brothers Live in Concert videotape. They had it hooked up to the stereo and were cranking it so the neighbors couldn't hear her on her knees breaking all the ten commandments of love. He could hear Aaron's voice singing sweetly as that nigger she was fucking stuck his finger in her ass laughing at the stupid picture of her husband standing proudly in front of the apartment he was at this moment tossing out the window, removing as he would an infected limb spilling its rot into the bloodstream of a body determined to survive, determined to survive by removing all remnants of infidelity still lingering in the air he breathed.

He went into his pocket looking for the lighter he introduced himself with. The lighter he lit her cigarette with before inviting her to his bedroom for that first time. The lighter he took from the unfamiliar pair of pants hiding underneath the bed he just tossed out the window. He figured it was the appropriate thing to start the fire that would burn anything he couldn't destroy by tossing out the window into the path of any moving vehicle. He flipped that lighter open and set fire to her underwear, her dresses, her shoes, and anything he thought had the possibility of one of that nigger's bleached-out cum stains. He let everything else burn just in case.

That was when he started thinking, what if he didn't fuck her on his bed? Elaborate pictures formed, and he was fucking her in the closet, in the living room, on the floor, each thrust moving her cheating ass along his double padded golden brown wall to wall carpet. He stepped out of the bedroom and he saw a thousand spots where they might have fucked, so he ran to the kitchen, found a steak knife and a pair of scissors, stabbed a hole big enough for the scissor blades, and with a detail unconscious of the fire growing in the bedroom, he cut out every potential fuck spot he saw, but as soon as he'd cut one, he'd suspect another one.

"He fucked her there. I know he did," he'd say, and he'd cut as the fire kissed the curtains away and cracked open the windows to burst outside. "He fucked her there. I know he did," he'd say and he'd cut as the fire slipped its fingers inside the linoleum and made goose pimples of the waxed tiles behind him.

"He fucked her there. I know he did," he'd say, and he'd cut as everything she'd ever touched in their bedroom burned secretly behind his back. When the firemen arrived, he was still burning in a position that appeared to make him unaware of the fire that creeped up his pant leg. He died kneeling, fighting desperately to cut that last spot out. He never made it back into the kitchen. If only he did, he probably would have noticed the cum stain pointing out the back door. Ain't no telling what he would have done then.

A Malicious Attack of True Love

She's pissing me off again, just like she always does, just like she knows she can. She's opening that window just a crack so the wind slips in and leaves a cold spot on my neck just below my hairline and just above where my favorite chair stops and I'm sitting, pissed.

"Goddamnit! Goddamnit, baby. Stop pissing me off. You know what I'm talking about. You're pissing me off again." She's pissing me off again, just like she always does, just like I let her do. She must have hidden some secret listening device on me, or I'm talking in my sleep, or she must have stumbled onto some ancient mind-reading technique, cause she always knows and she's plotting, plotting a way to make me say, "Goddamnit! Goddamnit, baby, why the fuck is my Coltrane tape under G? Where the fuck is my cheesecake, baby, you know I was saving that? What the fuck does this say? All I can read is the word 'important,' goddamnit!"

Goddamnit, baby, you're pissing me off. She's pissing me off, just like she always does, just like I know she will. I come home looking now, searching the walls for inconsistencies, blatant errors in my intricate organization, details written backwards just to piss me off. "What the fuck!" Goddamnit! Goddamnit baby, I'm getting ready. You're goddamn right there's hair in the sink. Hell fucking yeah the toilet seat's up. Damn straight I can hear you, I'm just ignoring you, goddamnit. Goddamnit, baby, you pissed me off, but I'm gonna piss my way back on.

SOMETHING IN THE RUINS

It was love, that's not what they called it on Vernon Avenue and Hoover Street, but it was love all right. It fit all the requirements, all the pleasure, all the pain, touch and need to touch. He gave her everything, the only thing he held dear, and she would do the same. Even on those cold nights, she would do the same. He would do the same.

They didn't call it love though, not on Vernon Avenue and Hoover Street. It was something else there. It was that too fat, too black, too ugly thing selling its too broken ass out in the back of the liquor store. It was that too funky, too dirty, too used fool begging to pump your gas for a dollar, wash your windows for a dollar, wipe your ass for a dollar.

It wasn't a man and a woman in a sleeping embrace. It wasn't two people sharing the addiction of pleasure, of pain, touch and the need to touch. It was just one of those Vernon Avenue and Hoover Street niggers, just one of those Vernon Avenue and Hoover Street whores. It was just the things nobody wants to touch.

And when he lights that pipe and gives her the first hit, and when they hit that rock together til there's nothing on the screen, and when they fall, warm, together, to Vernon Avenue and Hoover Street, it won't be called love. It will just be something that needs to be clean.

FOREPLAY IN THE NEIGHBORHOOD

She's "gonna blow up Parker Center," she says. She's "gonna put a bug in that computer of theirs, and set the whole world free." She's "gonna set me free." She's "a genius," she says. She's "past Einstein on the genius scale." And she's "gonna be my savior." She's "gonna blow up Parker Center" and I close my eyes. I can hear her talking, whispering in my ear, she's inside Parker Center. Her hand is in my pants, and she's pulling on that computer plug until everything blows, and L.A. doesn't have its teeth in me anymore. Everything blows, and Parker Center is just a hole in the ground in the middle of downtown.

She pulls that plug, whispers in my ear and there are ten thousand fools in blue wandering around looking for someone to fuck by the word of law, but I walk past. I can walk past. Parker Center is gone and I can walk past. "Remember" her name, she says. When you get pulled over next time, and they ain't got shit on you, remember. When they have to start again, when every time they touch you, it's illegal again. "Remember" her name. She's gonna pull that computer plug and black won't be an unlawful act anymore, so "remember her name."

I close my eyes. My pants are at my ankles. She's whispering in my ear. I remember her name, she's "gonna blow up Parker Center for me. She's "gonna be my savior," my dick is hard and I don't have to worry about that cop behind me anymore. I don't have to wonder if that cop knows about those one hundred million little nigger warrants placed on my naked black ass and preserved on all that fucking computer shit in Parker Center.

She's gonna blow up Parker Center. She's gonna be my savior. She's on top of me now and we're making what must be love cause I'm hiding inside her. I'm gonna hide inside her until she saves me, until she drops her bomb and saves me, until she blows up Parker Center like she said she would before she got my dick hard.

The Nigger in Flight

I wanted her to believe in me. I wanted her to look in my eyes and know, and believe I could fly. I wanted her to believe I could take that one extra step to outside, out a third story window. I wanted to show her that I was worth dreaming about, worth the tremendous effort it took to believe in me, to believe and see my wings.

I looked into her eyes, got up from the chair I was sitting in, the chair she saw my black ass sitting in all the time, the chair I wanted her to believe I could lift myself in flight from.

I got up and I looked into her eyes, took that chair and smashed the window, smashed the pane, the glass until I'd created an exit in the walls caging me, until see through barriers had been smashed, and the outside was blowing in to wherever my wings had to be. I stepped up into that window, up until I was standing, my feet upon reality, a step away from her dreams, my feet upon black, a step away from man, from angel. I stood in the window, crunching the broken glass beneath my feet, my hands cut and bleeding from the hidden slivers in the walls. I looked into her eyes searching for my wings, my invisible wings, my confined wings. I stood in the window. I looked into her eyes. I looked into her eyes. Her eyes said, "Jump, nigger." But I heard her say, "Fly."

THE THIEF

I only saw shadows. Then I saw her over there standing below the Billy Dee billboard on the side of that liquor store on 76th and Figeroa. I thought I saw her glowing, bright as an angel descended, fallen, but standing, selling, selling what the ground demystified and twisted into flesh and blood molded with a holy precision into female, needing, surviving.

I had to make three right turns to get my car to where I could see her again with her dirty blue jean skirt, bare legged down to her black Nikes with a purse stuffed fat with toilet paper and non-lubricated prophylactics dangling a half-smoked Marlboro Light between two fingers, she wasn't nothing special. And she would have remained a shadow had it not been for her brilliantly white t-shirt. It was her wings. It made her perfect. It made her an angel on 76th and Fig granting holy communion to any nigger passing with twenty dollars and a prayer for anything but anal absolution.

I parked about a hundred feet away from her and watched as the brake lights that should have passed untouched, got bright, then turned, and turned, and turned, to inquire. Occasionally she would vanish into idling automobiles with all of her necessities tucked away behind zipped or button-flied drudgeries containing stains in need of touch from the anchored wings of a crippled cherub. Occasionally she would leave for ten or fifteen minutes always returning to glow in the shadows below the neoned Pepsi sign with the 'J' from Joe's liquor store missing. She'd come back with a trick's worth of toilet paper and Trojans missing. She'd come back with her blue jean skirt a little more soiled or her Nikes a little more worn, but she'd come back with that t-shirt a little more perfect, a little brighter, untouched and angelic, she was an archangel, a cherub, a seraphim, only $20 from my touch and I knew I had to find out what made that t-shirt so white.

I knew I had to make my stain. I was gonna get my hands real dirty and touch her all over and in any cavity I selected. I was gonna get my hands real dirty and spit my crack smoke into the air she breathed, stir the dust from my PCP into a cloud surrounding her 76th Street shadows, spill my spoon-heated heroin into her pretty white cotton so deep that Clorox touched by the hand of God himself could not remove the permeating stench of her newfound morality.

I was gonna make my stain I was gonna get my hands real dirty and shoot my twenty dollars worth all over the places on her, in her that had to be touched by the hand of God. Descending to touch the Virgin Mary like white of a t-shirt glowing in the shadows rising past midnight.

I was gonna make a stain. I was gonna make my stain in the alley behind that liquor store behind the dumpster on anything broken enough to be considered garbage on 76th and Figeroa in Los Angeles. I was gonna make my stain in the Church's Chicken bathroom five blocks away in one of the pissed on, shit on, painted on stalls hiding in the shadows from the clean white hand of Our Lord in Heaven. I was gonna make my stain in any of the abandoned buildings beneath the city. I was gonna take her by her t-shirted wings and fuck her in the center of a room stinking of a nothing so institutionalized and perfect she would give a scream shrill enough to pierce the ears of any deity looking down and laughing at the niggers needing, surviving on the streets surrounding 76th and Figeroa. I was gonna make my stain. I was gonna make my stain. I was gonna make my stain and leave fingerprints all over her pretty glowing stain on my home. I was gonna make the world real again, touch black to the immaculate, turn wings to cotton, seraphim to whore.

But she saw me coming, unfurled her wings, and when I looked up past that fucked up Pepsi sign, that Billy Dee Schlitz Malt Liquor billboard, that sky at one time absent of her presence. When I looked up, fingers dirty, ready to make my stain all over her pretty little glow, when I looked up, I could see her rising, dropping shadows in her wake. I could see her rising, I could see her rising, ascending, or I blinked and she was gone.

"Until the day I die." That's what he'd been thinking for the past ninety days as he stepped out of the lock-up to place himself at her doorstep again, to wait for the police to arrive again. When they got there it would be the third time in recent memory that they'd taken him away, and as the time behind bars increased from a night in jail to a couple of nights in jail to thirty days in jail to the maximum amount of time allowed by law, he couldn't stop thinking about her, and he knew that when released he would be at her doorstep again, waiting, waiting, "Until the die I die."

He was thinking. "Until the day I die." He was praying, believing in the sacrifice made to be near her, but dreaming of a mercy that wasn't gonna come anymore, a mercy that wasn't worth the anger patrolling her neighborhood waiting for a call to explode by decree as he walked to her doorstep and sat down, waiting, listening to her footsteps trying to go about business as usual but gradually falling harder as the thought of him outside her door made her angrier and angrier.

"Go away," she'd say. "I'm gonna call the police," she'd say, but he would sit anyway. He would wait anyway. She wanted to be left alone. She wanted him to get the fuck out of her life, but he wouldn't go. He was gonna sit there. He was gonna sit there listening, waiting for the door to open and let him inside, for the door to open and her arms to wrap around him and beg forgiveness. He was waiting for the dream dreamt for the past ninety days to be as real as the sirens approaching, as the police gradually matching her anger, as the police releasing the clubs, unhooking the holsters, approaching a nigger in blatant defiance of the laws of twentieth century romance.

"Until the day I die," he thought as she finally came to the door after 123 days, fifteen minutes and twelve seconds.

"Go away," she said. "Please go away," she said, as the flash of the sirens turned the corner and she realized twenty-four hours had turned to ninety days and was about to become the black and white light flashing asskicking quickly approaching her doorstep. A tear formed and fell to her cheek, a tear she had found for a dog about to be beaten away from her life. He spoke to that tear.

"Until the day I die," he said. "I'll love you until the day I die," he said, in an alley a little more than two blocks away, about three feet from the squad car, after a little more than legally justifiable anger, and a fractured skull that was, incidentally, still thinking about her eyes, the day he was waiting for finally came.

THE AFTERTHOUGHT

"Pride," I said. I was heading for the door.

"I got pride," I said as I opened the door.

She wasn't gonna get my pride but she followed, screaming, "You ain't nothing. You ain't got money. You ain't got no job. You're worthless. You ain't a man. You're a child."

She followed, screaming, "You're a child. You ain't nothing. You ain't nothing." But I was walking away. My back was turned. I was walking away, thinking about my pride, thinking about pride pumping blood to my veins, the pride that kept my feet moving, the pride she opened her mouth to take a bite of again and again as she screamed the parts of me she'd chewed away to all the niggers forced to listen through the paper thin and falling apartment walls I was walking away from.

My back was turned. I was walking away as she screamed what I was, what I was not, and what she wanted to every nigger listening, ears pressed against every rat-holed and roach-infested insulation separating them from me and that bitch screaming, screaming, screaming. She screamed so every nigger listening could hear, so every nigger could hear, so every nigger was listening, and it was time to metamorphosize into the man of her dreams, or it was time to beat her motherfucking ass to within an inch of her life, or it was time to leave.

"Pride," I said. "I got pride," I said. She wasn't gonna get my pride. She wasn't gonna get my pride. My feet were moving. I still had my pride. My feet were moving. I still had my pride, and I left her alone and screaming, all bills due yesterday, no check in the mail, nothing to take, nothing to offer.

I left her alone and screaming and screaming in a building full of niggers with teeth sunk deeply into their pride, with mouths biting, attacking pride, ripping it away behind closed doors, closed fists, and "you ain't nothing." echoing at 2 a.m. in shit pink Section 8 tenement slum apartments with Raid and rust staining the inside walls and spraypaint staining the outside walls with names of children in search of something to pump the blood in their veins, of children in search of something to keep their legs moving, of children with teeth in their hearts, of children, of children.

I left her alone with our child in her arms. I left her alone so our child could hear. I left her screaming, and our child could hear. And our child could hear. Our child could hear, but the door was closed. "Pride," I said. "She wasn't gonna get my pride," I said, but the door was closed. Our child was in her arms. Our child was listening. "She wasn't gonna get my pride," I said. But the door was closed. Our child was in her arms, and she was gonna taste my blood. There was gonna be blood in her mouth.

WHERE THE EARTH MOVED

I called her when the walls collapsed to smash the dreams of sleeping children who were denied blessings in bedtime prayers only hours earlier, when the gaspipes leaked, the hiss ignited, and the sky exploded to blur horizon with fire. I called her when the land stuck its tongue in my ass and licked through cracks until I had to move, I had to shake, I called her when the water grew thick and red and tasted and smelled of her blood-cleansed mid-month cum. I called her when the world stopped breathing, the headlights stalled, the freeway opened and sucked freedom away. I called her when I believed hell had arrived. I didn't wait for it to freeze over like I said I would. I didn't want to burn without her hand in mine. I didn't want to burn alone, so I called her.

"Are you alright?" I said.

"I will be," she said.

"Then goodbye," I said. And the earth resealed, eventually. And the sky released itself from flames, eventually. And we all healed, eventually. And I hung up the phone. I never called her again.

SALVATION

"What do you believe in?" she asked. He looked up, then into her eyes. He was gonna answer. He'd never answered that question before. He never thought he had to. He never thought he had the right. He saw her belief as a crutch, a hand extended to balance a fall, arms to unite the falling. He had no right to take such beliefs, even to place question on such beliefs. Without her beliefs, she would fall. Without their beliefs, they would fall, but he was gonna answer her. Stand, he thought.

"You," he said, "I believe in you."

She came closer, held him, no crutches. That night it was over, but she would ask again. She saw him as falling. He hoped he would never lose his answer. It was so difficult to be alone and falling.

CRASH

I put the pen down empty, all lies on fire, burning pages naked of my truth, filled with dreams, fantasies, and prayers for hardened skin denied by a life of comfort, dignity, and forgotten memories alive for a second, impossible to capture forever in words.